The Freedman

Tales from a Revolution: North-Carolina

Also by Lars D. H. Hedbor,
available from Brief Candle Press:
The Prize: Tales From a Revolution - Vermont
The Light: Tales From a Revolution - New-Jersey
The Smoke: Tales From a Revolution - New-York
The Declaration: Tales From a Revolution - South-Carolina
The Break: Tales From a Revolution - Nova-Scotia
The Wind: Tales From a Revolution - West-Florida
The Darkness: Tales From a Revolution - Maine
The Path: Tales From a Revolution - Rhode-Island
The Tree: Tales From a Revolution - New-Hampshire
The Mine: Tales From a Revolution - Connecticut
The Siege: Tales From a Revolution - Virginia

The Freedman

Lars D. H. Hedbor

Brief Candle
Press

This is a work of historical fiction. Apart from the well-known actual people, events, and locales that figure in the narrative, all names, places, and incidents are products of the author's imagination or are used fictitiously.

Cover and book design: Brief Candle Press.
Cover image based on "Sunset on the Plains," Albert Bierstadt, 1887.
Map based on Claude Joseph Sauthier's Plan of the Town and Port of Brunswick in Brunswick County, North Carolina, 1769; reproduction courtesy of the Norman B. Leventhal Map Center at the Boston Public Library.
Fonts: Allegheney, Doves Type and IM FELL English.

First Brief Candle Press edition published 2018.
www.briefcandlepress.com

ISBN: 978-1-942319-29-0

Dedication

*For **all** of those who have joined in the struggle for freedom and justice, past and present*

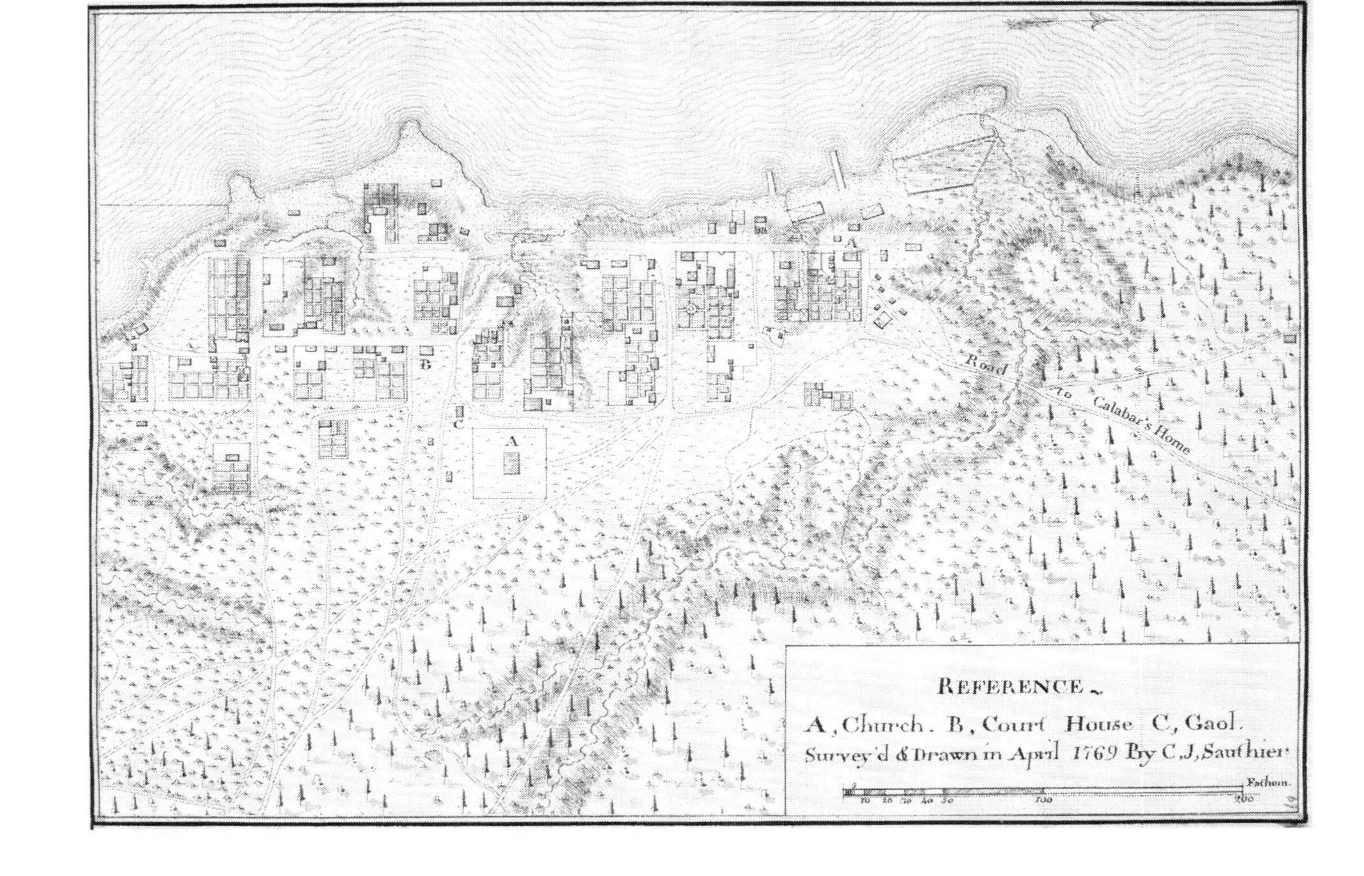

Road to Calabar's Home
A
B
C
A
REFERENCE ~
A, Church. B, Court House C, Gaol.
Survey'd & Drawn in April 1769 By C. J. Sauthier
10 20 30 40 50 100 200
Fathom

Linguistic Note

Most people who start to learn a new language after the age of about ten retain a noticeable accent all their lives; without intensive training, their speech patterns are likely to retain hints of the structure of their mother tongue as well.

I depict Calabar's English usage as haphazard when he is talking to people outside of his family and friends on the indigo farm where he grew up, while giving him normal colloquial usage when he was within that group. This was in part to convey that the communication barriers he faced were not shared with those with whom he was close, and in part to dispel the notion that he was simply unable to communicate clearly.

Chapter I

It was all over now. Calabar recognized the final rattle of breath from sitting by his own mother's deathbed, and he knew that his master's days were done.

Frederick Greene would never again rise from the mattress he had ordered Calabar to stuff with fresh straw earlier in the summer. The slave stood, reaching up to knead the tension out of his own shoulder, methodically thinking through what must be done next.

Mister Greene's son, a busy and prosperous tobacco farmer, must be summoned. Calabar felt the first stab of panic at that thought, as he did not trust what the younger Greene might decide to do with him, Affey, and their newborn daughter. He suppressed his fear, though, to focus on what must be done.

He ducked through the doorway of his master's bedroom, stepped out through the kitchen door and called out, "Affey! Come and help me saddle up Mister Greene's horse."

Affey appeared around the corner of the house, worry and fear written across her broad face. The baby was swaddled as usual in a sling against her chest, and she instinctively pulled her closer as she said in a quavering voice, "Is he . . . ?"

Calabar nodded solemnly. "I need to go and bring word to Master Greene. We must be ready to help him with whatever arrangements he will make for his father."

He grimaced, adding, "Master Greene . . . owns us now."

Affey's tears started in earnest now, though Calabar knew from the swirl of emotions that rampaged through his own heart that she wept not so much for their departed master as for the potential chaos that his death was sure to bring in its wake.

Calabar stepped forward and pulled her into his arms, but only for a moment. "We must be strong now, Affey. We cannot control what happens after this. We can only do what must be done. Right now, I need to ride that horse."

Affey nodded, wiping her tears away. She followed him to the stable and led the old mare out of her stall to blink lazily in the bright summer sunlight. Calabar was ready with the saddle, swinging it up onto the horse's back, and Affey wordlessly reached under the animal's belly to pass him the cinch.

He grunted in thanks and secured it, pulling it tight and waiting for the mare to exhale before tightening it completely. He ruefully remembered the only time he'd fallen for the horse's trick, and remembered, too the harsh words Mister Greene had lavished on him.

The master had returned, half an hour after the mare had ambled in, and Calabar was thankful that the man had had the long walk home to calm down a bit. If it had happened closer by, Calabar was reasonably sure that Mister Greene would have whipped him for his mistake.

As it was, his master had required Calabar to sweep and scrub the entirety of the stable until it gleamed, giving the slave no rest until the job was done. Calabar remembered few nights when he had been as grateful to fall into his bed of straw as that one, and even the full moon – high in the sky by the time he'd finished the job – could not keep him awake.

Shaking his head to dismiss the memory, Calabar slipped the bridle over the horse's head and slipped the bit between her teeth. He placed his foot into the stirrup as he'd seen Mister Greene do so many times, and attempted to swing himself up onto her back. He succeeded only in kicking her in the hindquarters, and she shied away, giving him a baleful glance over her shoulder.

Affey was struggling to keep a smile off her face, her lips pressed together in firm and serious determination, though her eyes told a wholly different story. Calabar sighed and said, "Fetch me that stool, if you could."

Stepping up onto the short stool, he tried again, and succeeded in getting himself up onto the saddle, albeit without his legs straddling the animal. Gracelessly, he scrambled into a seated position and worked his other foot into the stirrup.

Affey looked up at him. "Are you sure you should ride, and not just walk?"

He sighed, picking the reins up as he'd seen Mister Greene do on many occasions. "I may wind up walking. I should try to get there quick as I can, though."

He pulled the reins to one side, urging the horse to turn. She bent her neck in the direction he was pulling, but did not move her feet at all. He pulled harder, and the horse tossed her head and then started back for her stable, carrying Calabar along helplessly.

Affey followed, her expression no longer concealing mirth, but instead sharing in Calabar's obvious frustration. "Should I lead her back out?"

He shook his head in resignation. "I will just walk," he said, pulling his foot out of the stirrup and swinging it over the mare's back to jump down. "Can you remove the tack?" He got his other foot free of its stirrup and slid down to the ground.

She nodded and bent to start loosening the saddle, protecting the baby's head with one hand as she did so.

"Thank you, Affey. I had best set out. I will make up what time I can." He sighed again, grimacing. "I'll tell Shampee on my way. He will gather the others."

With no more than a quick glance back, Calabar set out down the road from the big house, between the fields grown waist-high on both sides of the road with the bushy indigo plants that had made Mister Greene so prosperous in life.

As he ran, he could hear the scream of a locust and smelled the damp earth of the fields. He breathed in deeply, glad that it was not yet harvest season – once the slaves began processing the indigo, the reek of the fermenting leaves would overpower everything else as far as the eye could see.

He approached the three-tiered processing vats and found Shampee, the plantation's slave driver, fetching water to bring to the crew working the field beyond the structure. He slowed to a walk, mastering his breath so that he could speak to the other slave.

Shampee looked up at Calabar's approach, concern clear in his expression. Mister Greene had been ill since the prior evening, and his condition had been a topic of conversation and speculation in the slave quarters far past the setting of the sun.

Calabar nodded in greeting to Shampee and said simply, "Mister Greene is dead. I'm going to go tell Master Greene. He will need to make arrangements."

Shampee's mouth fell open and, shaking his head slowly, he said, "Thought for sure that he was gonna pull through." His gravelly voice concealed any grief he was feeling, but he grimaced, betraying his emotions. "And just before the harvest, too."

Looking around at the indigo in the fields, Calabar agreed, "It's going to be a good crop, too. Shame Mister Greene didn't see it come in."

He motioned with his head back up the road. "I had best be off, Shampee. You gather the others and wait for Master Greene."

Shampee nodded. "Gonna be some changes here." He grimaced again and turned toward the fields, his steps mechanical.

Calabar returned to the road and followed the path to Master Green's plantation. He'd accompanied Mister Greene to his son's home several times, and knew the way well enough. It was a fair stretch, though, and by the time the large, well-kept house came into view, the sun was dipping visibly from its noontime zenith, casting lengthening shadows across the road.

He'd seen nobody else on the road – and a good thing, too, as he did not fancy being picked up as a runaway – but now, one of Master Greene's slaves spotted him and waved in greeting. Calabar dropped to a slow walk, his legs burning, and returned the wave.

The other man – an older, stooped slave whose name Calabar could not recall – hurried to him, asking, "Are you all right?"

Between breaths, Calabar puffed out, "I am fine, but I must speak to your master without delay."

Giving Calabar a quizzical look, the older man said, "He is in the house. I will take you."

They found Master Greene sitting at a large table, papers spread out before him in orderly piles. His face was broad and his characteristic shrewd expression gave way to a frown as he looked up to find Calabar standing before him.

"What brings you here, and in such a lather, boy?"

"I be so sorry, Master Greene. I got to tell you that your father done died."

Greene blinked quickly, his face registering shock, and he asked, "What? How? I just saw him a fortnight ago, and he was hale and hearty."

Calabar bowed his head, replying carefully, "He took ill quick at night, sir. He be weaker, weaker all night, then died just a while ago."

Greene cast his eyes downward toward his desk for a long moment before he replied, "This is an unlooked-for turn." He frowned again, saying almost more to himself than to Calabar, "What in the name of heaven am I going to do with an indigo plantation?"

Calabar kept his expression steady, but the fear that had burned in his gut ever since he saw Mister Greene's clammy, slack face by the light of the rising sun now roared into a blaze.

The questions came unbidden to his mind – would the slaves be sold, scattered like chaff in the wind? What would become of Affey and the baby? Could he persuade a new master to buy the three of them together? The routine of life on the indigo plantation was grueling, but it was familiar, and the prospect of having it snatched away by an untimely and sudden shift of fortune shook him to his core.

He realized that Master Greene was again gazing up at him, a thoughtful frown on his face. Greene called out to the older slave, who still stood behind Calabar in the doorway, "Albert, get the horses hitched to the cart, and make it fast."

Looking back at Calabar, he said, "I suppose you ran all the way here, then? Very well, you may ride to my father's plantation with me." He wrinkled his nose, adding, "You will sit on the back, however."

Chapter 2

Calabar had watched a handful of mourners come and go for Mister Greene's funeral, and was secretly glad that he did not have to suffer in the heavy black clothing they wore for the occasion.

At their new master's direction, Calabar and Shampee had maintained the routine of indigo culture, keeping the field slaves occupied with weeding the crops, maintaining the irrigation ditches, and picking pests from the valuable leaves.

Master Greene – he could not get himself into the habit of calling his new owner "mister" – did not concern himself with monitoring the indigo, unlike his father. Judging when the fields were ready to harvest was clearly going to be entirely in Calabar's hands. Tobacco was a wholly different business, and one with a rhythm that the younger Greene found more congenial.

A few days after his former master had been committed to the earth, Calabar entered the main house and was surprised to find his new master within, apparently waiting for him.

Greene asked, "Jupiter, isn't it?" His voice was flat and his eyes speculative as he regarded the slave.

"Yes, sir." His true name of Calabar he used only among his fellow slaves, and Mister Greene had informed him that he must answer to Jupiter in the confused and terrible days after the indigo farmer had purchased the boy and his mother at the dock.

Calabar was pulled away from those memories by Master

Greene's shrewd eyes meeting his own. "Your role here is to manage the extraction of the indigo dye from the plants at the end of the harvest?"

Calabar nodded, feeling the return of the lurch of fear in his gut, his regular companion. "That be right, sir. I help your father done that. He done taught me harvest. I be working the vats after harvest."

"And the rest of the year . . . ?"

Calabar swallowed hard. "I help gather, store seed. Some the time I be driving instead Shampee. I also be –"

Greene held up a hand abruptly, silencing him. "Have you any skills not related to the indigo?"

Calabar shook his head slowly. "No, sir. Indigo be what your father grow. It be what I always done."

Greene's mouth worked into an elaborate frown.

"How long do you figure it is liable to be until the harvest begins, then?"

Calabar shrugged. "Might be soon as tomorrow. Might be longer. Plants be big enough, but the leaves don't yet be turned."

Greene shot him a skeptical look, and Calabar hurried to explain. "When I be crushing leaf, it be turning blue when harvest be ready." He raised a hand to demonstrate crushing a leaf between his fingers.

Greene waved dismissively. "I need not know the details; I shall have to rely on your experience in this matter. How soon after the harvest is the dye reduced and ready for market?"

"Might be fortnight, might be ten day. It be depending on heat."

Greene's eyes narrowed, and Calabar hastened to explain

further. "Indigo bricks must be dry. Hot weather, no rain, make that faster."

Greene now nodded brusquely. "I see. And after the dye is reduced, you busy yourself with seed for the next season?"

Calabar nodded. "This be the second harvest. Shampee's crew be setting aside the pods. They be drying, then I –"

Again, Greene stopped him with an upraised palm. "I said that I do not need to know how you go about your every little task here. I am but trying to develop an understanding of how you earn your keep on the plantation."

He shook his head. "I have learned what I needed. I presume that you entered the house on some errand, and I do not wish to detain you any longer than is necessary from your work." He waved his hand dismissively. "You may be on your way, Jupiter."

Calabar said, "Yes, sir. Thank you, sir," nodding vigorously, and hurried past the other man into the kitchen.

There, he found Affey on her hands and knees, scrubbing out the firebox of the great hearth of the kitchen. The sopping rag in her hands was even darker than her skin, and she did not hear him enter over the sound it made as it swept over the sooty brick of the hearth.

The baby was slung snugly against her chest, and as she worked, he could hear her crooning softly to their daughter. "Just a little more, just a little longer," she said, craning her neck to kiss the crown of the baby's head.

As she did so, she spotted Calabar out of the corner of her eye, and jumped in surprise at seeing him.

"How long you been there?" she said, sitting back and mopping her brow with her hand, leaving a broad smudge of soot.

He shrugged. "Just talked to Mister Greene." He could keep the tremor out of his voice as he added, "I think he means to sell me. He wanted to know when the harvest is done. Asked a lot of questions about what I know, what I do all year."

Affey jumped to her feet and rushed over to embrace him. "Oh, Calabar, tell me it ain't so!"

He wrapped an arm around her and rested his cheek on top of her head.

"Nothing we can do about it, Affey. It's the way of things. He loves growing tobacco, probably more than old Mister Greene loved indigo."

Stepping away from her, he surveyed the kitchen, noting that it was in a general state of disarray, quite strange to see in her domain. "What is going on here?"

She followed his glance around the room at the heaped utensils, pots, knives, and serving dishes. "Mister Green, he told me to count up all the things. Then he said to put the place to right, just like it was new-built."

Calabar snorted. "This kitchen is nearly twenty years old. There's no way to make it all new."

"I know, I know. I can make it a pretty sight, though. Maybe if it's good enough, he'll want to move here from his old house."

Calabar favored her with a skeptically cocked eyebrow.

"Well, it can't hurt to try," she said, defensively. "I must feed Fantee," she said, changing the subject. "Been putting her off for a while, but she's fussing."

He nodded, and as she arranged the baby to suckle, he remembered what had brought him to the main house in the first place.

"Shampee sent me to get a poultice from you for old Hal. His knee is acting up again. With things being the way they are . . . "

She interrupted with a grimace, "He doesn't want to look infirm." She nodded emphatically. "Just as soon as I am done here, I will get one together for him."

"Do you need anything gathered?"

She looked up at the ceiling for a moment, thinking, and then turned back to him. "Check to make sure that we have some tobacco leaves."

He smiled grimly. "Tobacco we have in plenty. Master Greene brought a fresh supply with him."

She returned his tight smile, saying, "The rest I know I have. Tell Shampee that Hal will have his poultice at dinner time."

"I will tell him." He turned to leave through the back door, intent on avoiding another encounter with Master Greene.

"And Calabar?"

"Yes, Affey?" He stopped, looking at her expectantly.

"We will be all right, no matter what happens. We will take care of our baby, and each other. All Master Greene can do is tell us what our bodies must do. Our hearts are still our own."

Calabar paused for a moment, then nodded and went outside.

Chapter 3

Calabar walked wearily into the slave quarters, scarcely able to put one foot after the other. He could no longer smell the foul reek of the indigo vats on his skin, but he knew it clung to him like a fogbank cresting a ridge.

His crew had finished up with the beater vat by torchlight, as the liquid in it had performed its now-familiar magic. The slaves had worked the mechanical paddles – grateful for the modern innovation that made the work go faster – for hours, until the stinking effluent of the steeping vat had turned green in color, and then a deep blue.

Another hour or so of gentler paddle work, and the blue had started to settle. In the morning, they would draw off the water that stood over the sediment, and then scoop out the indigo mud and put it into hempen bags to drain even further.

Tomorrow, they would pour the drained indigo mud into forms to shape bricks for market, which was relatively easy work. A week or so in the sun, if the weather continued fair and hot, and the harvest would be done for the year. Calabar shook his head to himself as he walked. He felt certain that he was working himself out of a job, and despite Affey's brave words, the warm flames of fear were never far from flaring up in his gut.

He was too weary to consider the matter further, though, and gingerly settled himself down beside Affey's sleeping form. The baby woke and fussed, but by the time Affey had quieted her by giving her suckle, he was already asleep.

He awoke, as usual, with the crowing of the rooster at sunrise. Of course, several of the roosters liked to crow, and they did so at all odd hours, but the cock of the walk – a gaudy, strutting bird with a brilliant iridescent green tail – had a distinctive call, and, more important to Calabar's purposes, a reliable habit of waiting for the sun to crest over the eastern horizon before giving voice to his alarum.

Calabar's arms still ached from yesterday's hard physical work, but he knew that they were past the worst of it now, and what remained was more tedious than laborious. Affey was already up, of course, stoking the hearth in the main house for the day's baking and cooking, as well as the open fire in the slave kitchen, an outdoor space near their quarters.

Once the master was fed, she would collect some of the sweet potatoes – almost identical to the yams Calabar remembered from his early childhood, before he and his mother had been captured and loaded onto the ship – and put them in the coals. The collard greens were a little past their best flavor, but the garden he helped her maintain beside the quarters was still full of their bushy, dark green leaves, so he knew that she'd get out the old iron pot and boil up some of those, too.

During previous harvests, old Mister Greene sometimes supplemented their rations with rice from his cousin's plantation, but young Master Greene had apparently never heard of this practice, so the big pot would, as usual, be filled with ground hominy corn, and lots of it. Last night, Affey had even slaughtered an old hen that had quit giving eggs, and the crew had eagerly slurped at the soup she'd brought them at the vats.

The other field hands were stirring as Calabar went out into the low, slanting sunlight of the morning, but Shampee would see to getting them out to the vats in good time. Meanwhile, Calabar walked through the morning quiet, alone with his shadow, which stretched out along the way before him.

Without conscious thought, his nose wrinkled as he came within smelling distance of the vats. The odor was, as every year, overwhelming, and he paused to wait for a spasm of coughing to pass as he let his chest become accustomed to the bad air that lingered about the vats.

When he could breathe normally again, he continued to the bags, reaching out to feel the consistency of each as he passed. He nodded to himself, satisfied. He wiped his stained fingers on his legs and onto his garments, noting the streaks of clear, bright blue they left across the rough grey cloth.

It was truly a shame that Mister Greene had not lived to see this harvest. The indigo was, perhaps, of the highest quality Calabar had ever seen, and he felt a small, fierce pride in the knowledge that this was due to his own experience and knowledge.

Without him, Shampee could probably have managed to produce a harvest that would have been acceptable in the marketplace, but this indigo would be able to fetch a top price in the market. He remembered Mister Greene telling him how the bricks were split into ever-smaller slivers of pure dye, and then sold for fantastic prices in Boston and Philadelphia, and even far-off London.

Mister Greene's prosperity sometimes even reached the slave quarters, whether in the form of some rice, or a bolt of cloth to make new shifts for the field slaves, or even – one memorable year – pairs of worn, but perfectly usable shoes for both Calabar and Shampee.

Shampee had worn his shoes out before the end of the next harvest, as he delightedly pranced about in them constantly, but Calabar still had his pair, and only wore them on special occasions, when he wanted to remind Affey that she had picked the only man from among the slaves who had a proper pair of shoes.

Of course, he had no expectation that their new master would shower them with such largesse. His throat tightened into another spell of coughing, and he fought to overcome both the bad air and the hot coal of fear that had flared again in his heart.

Catching his breath, he turned to inspect the forms that had already been laid out to receive the indigo mud, leaning down to straighten some, and lifting others to tap out debris that still clung to their sides from the last harvest. As he set one of the forms down after clearing it out, he spied a boy running down the track that led to the main house.

He set the form back in place carefully and stood, waiting for the boy's arrival. Calabar smiled when he saw that it was Shampee's youngest, a spindly child who could not carry a load like his father, but could run faster than most anyone else around.

The boy puffed to a stop in front of Calabar and said breathlessly, "Master Greene wants you up at the big house."

Calabar could see him register the stench of the vats and it seemed to remind him to add, "He said that you ought to bathe before you come, too." Affecting the clipped accent of the young Master Jones, the boy added, "He cannot abide the smell of the indigo."

Calabar smiled at the boy's impression of the master, and

gave him a friendly jostle on the top of the head. "I will need to stop by the stream before I go up. See that he knows that I am on my way."

As the boy raced back toward the main house, the smile on Calabar's face faded, and he trudged dully toward the stream. No good could ever come of a summons to the presence of a master such as young Mister Greene.

Having performed the necessary ablutions, Calabar reported dutifully to the spacious study in the main house, knowing that Mister Greene had favored the view across his fields that its windows afforded. Like his father had once done, Master Greene stood surveying the plantation in the morning light.

Without turning away from the windows, he said, "Jupiter, you have been here since before I left to establish my own plantation. In all of those years, you have not learned any useful trade outside of the processing of indigo."

Calabar stood mute, the tone of finality in Master Greene's voice clearly telling him that the time for protestations and argument was past – if, indeed, there had ever been such an opportunity.

Greene continued, "I have taken the decision to convert my father's plantation to the production of tobacco, as it is a better use than indigo of the land and of the labor I have inherited from him."

Calabar felt his heart pounding against his ribcage, and was exquisitely aware of every blood vessel in his body as he waited for the fatal words he anticipated.

Greene turned and faced him, his expression tight and dour. "Since I can make no use of you, and I have found no indigo plantation with need for your services, I have decided to simply send you on your way, to discover what fortune your freedom may permit you."

Turning back to the window, and leaving Calabar struck dumb behind him, he added, as if in an afterthought, "Leave now; I want you off my land before your fellows break fast this morning. The indigo harvest is complete, and I cannot see the sense in having you stay to stir up trouble among my slaves."

Calabar found his voice and stammered out, "Wh-what be happening with Aff – I mean, Anna, and our child?"

Greene's voice was colder and firmer than before, if that were even possible. "I said, leave now." Without even bothering to look back at Calabar, he pointed behind himself to the door, and in Greene's reflection on the window, Calabar could see his mouth set in a firm, determined line.

Feeling as though his arms and legs were made of lead, or were caked in a thick sludge of indigo mud, Calabar turned slowly, mechanically and left his entire life behind.

Chapter 4

As the sun rose high into the sky – he couldn't help but think that it was ideal weather for the next step in drying the indigo mud into bricks for market – Calabar continued walking, letting the easy, mindless motion numb his whirling thoughts.

He remembered the night that Affey had labored and birthed Fantee. A great storm had broken over the plantation, washing down the lingering odor from processing the first harvest this year. Though the lightning flashed and the thunder roared, its voice calling back and forth between the surrounding hills, Affey's cries had brought more apprehension to Calabar's heart.

When the toothless old woman who had midwifed for her had emerged from the dark corner of the slave quarters where Affey had been brought to labor, a broad smile on her face had given Calabar the gift of breath again. She had nodded, her eyes twinkling at his eagerness, and said in her soft lisp, "You have a fine daughter. Affey has named her Fantee."

The old woman had endured Calabar's embrace, and he could almost feel her approving gaze in the darkness as he made his way to Affey's side. The lightning guided him around a puddle where the rain streamed through the roof, to where Affey lay, the baby lying on her breast.

It was fitting somehow, that his first glance at his daughter had been lit by a flash of lightning. It was but the blink of an eye since her birth, and now she and Affey were ripped away from him forever. Calabar refused to permit himself to feel any shame for the tears that streamed down his face, though they left him scarcely able to see any better in the daylight than he had on that stormy night.

He had long since passed out of the boundaries of Mister Greene's plantation, and walked along an open road, his destination completely unknown to him. A persistent mosquito paced him, occasionally whining into one ear and then the other. A sharp sting on his forehead informed him that his tormentor had found its mark, and he swatted it flat without a thought.

The bright splash of blood on his fingers gave him a moment of exasperation, and he impatiently wiped his forehead clean with the back of his hand, drying his eyes in the same motion. He shook his head angrily, his mind racing through a variety of things that he might have done differently.

He thought back to the day that old Mister Greene had taken him aside during the harvest, saying, "Boy, you seem to have an eye for keeping your bricks neat, and not much back for the labors of the harvest. How would you like to learn to judge the vats, and be spared the fields?" If only he had declined, and worked to overcome his gangly legs and arms . . .

Or the first visit to young Master Greene's plantation, accompanying the elder Greene on a visit to purchase a pair of new slaves. One had been a shy girl, about his own age, introduced as "Anna," and Calabar had smiled at her reassuringly as the masters had completed her sale. Perhaps he should have turned away, instead . . .

Or, most recently, when Master Greene had asked what Calabar knew, beyond the indigo, he could have invented skills and knowledge that would have been more appealing to a tobacco farmer, and might have convinced his new master to make a place for him . . .

Calabar sighed deeply. None of these things had happened, though, and he had known in his heart that his fate was already sealed, even before the harvest had begun.

He had expected to be sold, though – with luck, to the same buyer as Affey, or ideally, to a new owner for the entire indigo plantation. He had never imagined being cast out on his own, to find his way in a world that offered little to his kind.

He stopped on the road, feeling his breath rush in and out of his chest, and pondered what he might do next, where he ought to go. He had heard from others stories about freed slaves, that they found ways to scratch out a living, but that those who failed to comply with a myriad of complicated and seemingly unknowable rules were subject to being seized and returned to slavery.

These were problems for later; in the moment, he needed to find some means of providing food for his belly – he suppressed the awareness of its grumbles – and a roof over his head, but he had no idea of how to go about earning his way, or what the steps were of those fortunate few who had escaped both slavery and starvation.

As he stood there thinking, a wagon pulled by two fine, proud bays rounded the corner ahead. Calabar resisted the urge to duck off the road and try to conceal himself in the tall grass – he realized, with a fresh shock, that he had as much right as anyone to stand on the road and greet the two men on the wagon.

As they approached, he saw that they looked alike enough

to be twins, and both of them were regarding him with outright suspicion.

One called out as the other brought their wagon to a halt, "Boy, where are you bound to on this fine morning?"

Calabar's mouth felt dry, and he stammered out in answer, "I – I have not decided, sir."

The man crooked his eyebrow at Calabar and elbowed his companion. "You hear that, Jake? A negro who thinks he decides where he'll go?"

Turning back to Calabar, he said, "Boy, what makes you think that you get to decide?"

"Sir, I been freed by my master this morning."

It was Jake's turn to cock a skeptical eyebrow in Calabar's direction. "John, that is an unlikely sounding story." He made a show of looking Calabar over. "What master would turn loose a likely looking specimen such as this boy, without he has done something worthwhile?"

John chimed in again. "Did this master of yours give you your walking papers?"

Calabar's face must have registered his confusion, for John added, "Your manu – manimiss – ah, donkey spit, the papers that say that you're a free man."

Jake added helpfully, "Manumission."

"Yeah, those. You got 'em?"

Calabar's heart sank. "No, sir, I do not. He been told me leave, that there be no place for me anymore, I be leaving." Inwardly, Calabar was scarcely surprised to learn that his freedom was defective, that his status was even more precarious than he had thought.

John gave him a reproachful look. "You honestly expect us to believe that tall tale? Jake, I don't believe him, do you?"

Jake said to Calabar, "Who is this master of yours, what sent you on your way without so much as a written-down by-your-leave?"

"He be Franklin Greene, his Pa been Frederick Greene." Calabar felt the name grate against his teeth as he uttered it.

Jake's eyes narrowed. "Aye, I've heard about Frederick Greene's sudden departure from this life. Franklin's a level-headed man, though one who doesn't let so much as a shilling squeeze through his fingers without it has given a little yelp."

He gave Calabar a look of cool appraisal. "Boy, I am inclined to join with my brother John in his disbelief of your story. Your master's plantation isn't so much out of our way, so how about you hop on up here and we'll go pay Franklin a visit, to discover the truth of the matter."

"No, sir, Mast – I mean, Mister Greene would not be liking that. He been eager to see me gone." Calabar could feel the sweat bead up on his forehead at the prospect of having to face Greene again.

Jake eased back the front of his traveling cloak and put his hand on the butt of a pistol it had concealed. "I don't think you understand, boy. You will be coming back with us to the Greene plantation, one way or another."

John's eyebrows danced on his forehead as he struggled to contain his mirth. "We've got a negro here who thinks he has all manner of choices, don't he?"

Jake let his cloak drop back and made a shushing motion at his brother with his hand. "What'll it be, boy? Are you gonna jump on up in back, or wait for my brother and me to heave you up there with a hole in you?"

It didn't seem like Calabar's shoulders could fall any further, but he felt them slump as he nodded and walked to the back of the wagon. It was empty of cargo, and he sat down silently on it, his legs dangling over the back.

John called back over his shoulder, "Boy, I think I'd like it better if you was to sit right up close here, where I can keep an eye on you."

Calabar stood on the bed of the wagon, and as he started to walk forward, he saw, too late, John give a twitch of the reins, causing the horses to start and the wagon to lurch into motion beneath him. He fell gracelessly, skinning his knees and palms on the rough wood of the wagon bed.

John chortled, even as his brother shot him a disapproving look. "Oh now, Jake, I didn't mean nothing by it. He ain't hurt, are you, boy?"

Calabar said nothing, but sat up and settled himself against the low-slung side of the wagon, looking dully at the fields passing slowly by as the wagon now retraced his leaden steps away from the plantation.

In what seemed like a mere moment of time, the wagon had jolted past the vats, where Calabar could see Shampee guiding the crew through the pouring of the indigo bricks, and past the slave quarters, where he realized with a pang that his shoes still lay, lost to him forever. It pulled up before Greene's big house, where Calabar knew that Affey must by now know of his fate, and had only Fantee to comfort her.

Jake turned to Calabar, asking, "What is your name,

boy?"

Without looking at the man, Calabar answered in a flat voice, "Jupiter, sir."

Jake nodded. "Well, Jupiter, you stay here with John while I go and find out whether there is a reward for your return, or if you've lied about where you come from."

Calabar could not even find the energy to object to the man's assumptions. "Yes, sir."

John twisted around in his seat and grinned merrily at Calabar. "Hope it's a good reward. I could use the money for a nice bottle of rum." He gave Calabar a hard poke on the shoulder, but the miserable man didn't give him the satisfaction of a response.

Bored, John turned back to survey the plantation, though he kept Calabar within his line of sight. Clearly, he had his heart set on that bottle of rum.

Calabar did his best to not look around, not wanting to sharpen the pain in his gut by catching sight of – or being seen by – any of his former companions on the plantation. A fly, drawn to the salt of his sweat, landed on his brow, and Calabar could not even summon the willpower to shoo it away.

The minute tickle of the creature's feet as it walked over his skin gave Calabar something to focus on besides the plantation, or his rowdy captor, or his uncertain future. His eyes came to rest on a knot in the wood of the wagon bed, and he let his focus slip into blurriness as he waited for his fate.

The crunch of footsteps approaching shook him out of his mindless reverie, and he looked up to see Jake walking back to the wagon, carrying a folded paper in his hand.

He offered it to Calabar, saying, to John's amazement,

"Jupiter here was telling us the truth. He is a free man, and Franklin corrected his oversight in not previously writing out a manumission on the spot."

Jake gave Calabar a look of what might have been pity. "Should you like to help us load up the wagon at our destination, I would be willing to give you supper when we get back to town. Beyond that, I cannot offer you employment, but I can direct you to some men who might have use for you."

John gaped at his brother, who shrugged. "Greene was most concerned that we get the boy off his plantation immediately. As for the rest, another set of hands will make the work faster, and that's worth a plate of food to me."

John scowled. "Yeah, but some help with the load doesn't get me any rum, now, do it?"

Jake did not answer, but climbed up to his seat and took up the reins, guiding the cart away from the plantation and toward Calabar's uncertain future.

Chapter 5

Loading the cart had been the work of a sweaty afternoon, though Calabar had to ignore the barbs thrown his way by John - still resentful of the bottle of rum he'd hoped to earn by turning in an escaped slave – as well as the unfriendly glances from passers-by and laborers in town.

After they secured a piece of canvas over the load, Jake led his brother and Calabar to a public house, where he had the freedman wait outside. He came back out in a moment with half a loaf of bread and a slab of hard cheese, which he pushed into Calabar's hands.

"Ain't much, but it'll keep body and soul together for another day," he said, smiling at Calabar. "Now, if you were an enterprising fellow, you'd make the acquaintance of Old Joe at the merchantile. He's always belly-aching about not having enough boys about to load goods into his warehouses."

Calabar sniffed the cheese and wrinkled his nose, stifling a sneeze at its sharp reek. "Old Joe," he repeated. "Be at merchantile."

"Aye, and if he's got nothing for you, there's always work at the docks, though you'll want to stay clear of the drunks and the other sad cases down there. Someone offers to throw bones with you, you just tell them you ain't got money, and they'll lose interest but quick."

Calabar nodded, though he wasn't quite sure what the man meant about bones and money.

Jake grinned at Calabar. "You'll be fine, boy, and if you ain't, why, I'm sure that the sheriff won't mind selling you back into service, by and by."

Calabar scowled. Though he had no idea yet what he might do with his freedom, he found that he was not eager to have it taken away. Jake clapped him on the shoulder. "Good luck to you. You always put in an honest day's work like you did on the cart this afternoon, you'll stay on the right side of the law."

The man turned and re-entered the tavern, leaving Calabar standing in the sun, with his bread and cheese and more questions than he had answers.

The first question was posed with some urgency by the rumble of his empty belly. He took a bite of the bread, and found with some surprise that it was fresh. He had had bread before – Affey had seen to that – but it was always scraps left from loaves a day or two old. This one had seen an oven this very day, and the texture was far softer than he was accustomed to.

He ventured a nibble at the cheese, which was a complete novelty. Affey had described it to him before, but she ran her kitchen too well for any to ever go to waste, so none had ever come home with her. It was salty and had a sour creaminess that he was at first unsure of, but he found himself nibbling at it again, almost without thinking about it.

The door to the tavern opened, and a man regarded him with a suspicious glare. "What are you hanging about for? Move along, and don't let me catch you asking honest people for nothing, you hear me?"

Calabar nodded wordlessly and walked away down the hard-packed street. He'd not looked around much when Jake had led him here, and had only been here a few times before, but now he examined the town with frank interest.

The buildings were huddled close together, as though for friendly company with one another, with homes close by shops of all sorts. A few people moved about, most of whom seemed to not really see him as he passed. Those who did see him either gawped with open curiosity, or else scowled, as though his presence were an affront to the orderly surroundings.

He turned a corner and noted that there was a narrow alleyway behind the row of buildings he'd been walking along, where another row that backed up to them. In the shadowed space between the rows of buildings, he saw a flicker of movement as a boy ran along, a package clutched to his chest. The boy disappeared into a back door in one of the buildings, and Calabar got the first inklings of an idea of how he might earn another meal after this one was exhausted, if Old Joe didn't want his help.

Surely in a town like this, there would be parcels that needed to be moved about, and Calabar had always been a quick study of faces and names. He frowned, though, as he realized that boys like the one he'd seen probably already met those needs. Still, it couldn't hurt to ask one of them.

He nodded to himself, the food in his stomach restoring some of his optimism. For the first time since Master Greene had summoned him into the house, he started to feel as though he might find a way to survive the strange new circumstance of freedom.

By the time the sun was setting, Calabar was no longer so sure of that. When he'd found his way to the merchantile, Old Joe had dismissed him offhand. "Got enough boys these days, between hands jumping ship and farmers giving up and coming into town, no need to add another negro to stir things up."

Opportunities at the docks had been no more promising, and had smelled, if anything, even worse than the worst indigo vat.

He'd drifted back to the public house, and when the same man as before emerged to find him sitting on the bench outside, Calabar had cringed as though expecting a blow. The tavernkeeper grimaced at the sight of the freedman, then looked him over shrewdly.

"Were I to offer you another meal, could you shift some goods about for me in the back?"

Calabar nodded. "Show me what be need done."

"Come around through the alley and I'll meet you back there." The tavernkeeper closed the door, and Calabar rose wearily to his feet. Even as much as he walked in the course of a normal day working the indigo, he had gone much further than usual today.

When he reached the back of the tavern - he counted the buildings as he passed them on the front, and then the back, to be sure he was going to the right one - the tavernkeeper emerged from its back door. He pointed to a stack of barrels. "Those are all empty, and the man who was supposed to take them away never showed up today."

The tavernkeeper scowled. "They're in the way now, as I'm expecting a delivery tomorrow, presuming that someone around here can keep a promise. You move them from there to here" – he indicated a spot on the far side of the doorway – "and I'll feed you supper. Mind that you handle them gently – crack the staves and

I'll get no credit at all for them. Suits?"

Calabar nodded again. "It be done before dark."

The work had taken him only a little time, but it had added to the ache in his back and the overwhelming weariness in his limbs. The meal - another half-loaf of bread and a small, bitter apple - had settled his stomach a little, but now he was faced with the question of where he might bed down.

The alleyway was, at least, partially sheltered, and after the tavernkeeper went back inside, Calabar sat down to eat with his back to the stack of barrels he'd moved.

Would every day be like this? On the plantation, he'd known where he needed to be, even if he had no choice in the matter. Now, he couldn't seem to even find anyplace where he would be permitted to be for any amount of time. Was his freedom only to be the the freedom to slowly starve? He was still pondering these questions when sleep claimed him, still leaning against the barrels and the back wall of the tavern.

Chapter 6

"Are you the one called Jupiter?" The merchant's eyes were shrewd, and his waistcoat stretched tightly over a gently ample gut. Calabar looked up at him in surprise.

"Yes, sir, that be my name." He sat on a low bench, outside of the public house where he had been irregularly employed – and fed, though the tavern keeper would not suffer him to be housed within – since his ejection from the plantation.

The merchant nodded, rubbing his neck with one hand as he stifled a yawn with the back of the other. Calabar suppressed the urge to yawn in reply.

The merchant shook his head violently, as though trying to shake away a fly, but Calabar could see no pest on him. The other man held up his index finger for a moment, shaking it in a gesture asking for patience as his face screwed up, presaging a violent sneeze.

He stood for a moment more, regaining his composure, and muttered, "Sorry, the snuff took longer than I expected to do its business. Blasted stuff is a necessary evil, as it helps clear out the humors, but it can lead to ill-timed results."

Calabar nodded politely, as though he understood, though he had no idea what the man was talking about.

Beginning again crisply, the merchant said, "I am given to

understand that you know a bit about indigo. Is that the case?"

Calabar thought for a long moment, unsure of what the man was getting at. The past weeks had been among the worst he could remember, almost as bad as the cramped, stinking shipboard passage from his home to what had been then, and was now again, a bewildering and terrible land. Even a relatively simple question such as this was . . . difficult.

"Yes, sir, I been most of my life working the vats."

The merchant's eyes narrowed as he looked Calabar over cooly. "Have you the judgment to be able to tell a superior brick of indigo apart from one that is merely acceptable? I warn you, much relies upon this knowledge, should you claim it."

"Yes, sir, I think I have. You got wait for ferment be done, then you got choose the right time to –"

The merchant held up his hand and shook his head. "Though it is a subject of some fascination, I do not need to learn right at this moment all that there is to know about the production of the indigo, just whether you can look at a brick of the stuff and tell me what its quality is."

Calabar's brow beetled as he nodded. "Yes, sir, I be able to do that." He stopped talking, as it was clear that like most people not directly involved in the process, this man did not want to be bothered with more detail than a simple answer to his initial question.

The merchant rubbed his nose vigorously, then gestured to Calabar, pointing the way down the street. "Excellent. Come with me then. I need your advice on some indigo that I am thinking of buying, for shipment on tomorrow's departure for London."

"Yes, sir." Calabar stood, following the merchant as he

walked nearly as quickly as he spoke.

"I've no time to waste, but I've had a standing order from a factor in London for top-quality indigo for some time, and I dare not send any but the best, that I might retain his trust. Despite my inquiries, I've found nobody else knowledgeable about the indigo who isn't trying to sell it to me, or else bid against me for it. As I know nearly nothing of the stuff, I've not attempted to fill his order, but when I heard from a customer that there was a freedman newly in town from the indigo plantations, I knew at once that this could be a solution to my problem."

Calabar nodded, feeling for the first time in better than a fortnight some glimmer of hope. He patted the folded paper he kept tucked in his tunic, reassuring himself that it was still there. He could feel his ribs through the already well-worn page, and wondered whether helping this man would put some food in his aching belly.

The merchant had gone on talking, and Calabar struggled to keep up with his pace, both in steps and words. "I have the choice of a handful of suppliers from the country about here who are all bringing indigo to market, and sufficient capital to make a deal with all possible haste. If your knowledge of the indigo is what I hope it to be, I shall not want for capital again for some time, despite the late troublemaking in Boston-town."

He stopped suddenly in the street and fixed Calabar with an intense expression. "Mind you, I am not insensible to the complaints they have raised there – a man likes his tea without the bitter aftertaste of injustice – but I cannot help but think that there may have been more productive ways to have gone about voicing their displeasure with the Parliament."

He resumed walking just as briskly as before, and Calabar, utterly at a loss to understand half of what the man was talking about, again followed, bewildered, in his wake. He had heard, of course, of Boston, but had no conception of what a thing called a 'parliament' might have to do with tea, which was nearly as foreign to him as that far-off town.

While he mused over these thoughts, the trader seemed to be lost in his own pondering for a brief moment of respite. Almost to himself, he added, "Of course, if that formidable Missus Barker has anything to say about it, we shall all be forced to drink ditch water before we may resume the healthful and wholesome habit of tea, only because it is stained with the mark of England."

He turned back to face Calabar, a smile quirking on his face. "I imagine that you do not concern yourself with such matters when you take your tea, confining your considerations to the simple questions of how much cream and how much sugar you would like in it."

Calabar answered honestly, "Sir, I never been drinking tea, but my old master been drinking it plenty." Remembering Affey's amusement at Mister Greene's habits, he added, "He some of the times took it with a little rum, but there always been plenty of cream in it."

The merchant seemed struck dumb in disbelief when Calabar pronounced his innocence of tea, but broke into a wide grin at the mention of rum. "I must confess, Jupiter, that it had never occurred to me to put rum to my tea, as I like both well enough on their own, but I will have to try that the next time that the opportunity presents itself."

He shook his head and continued walking briskly, calling

over his shoulder to Calabar, "As for yourself, well, you look as though you could do with some feeding up and tea is just the thing to stimulate the appetite and ensure that you eat all that is set before you." He patted his rotund belly and said, "As you can see, it has worked wonders for my constitution."

He stopped suddenly again, but this time in front of a large, covered pavilion where various farmers and merchants were engaged in haggling over the goods stacked within. "Here we are, now. I believe we will find several farmers have delivered their indigo to the market this morning, and we have but to select the best of the lot – assuming that any are worthwhile at all – and then we may retire for a meal, if you should like."

Calabar felt his stomach twist at the thought of food – a real meal! – but he felt compelled to ask cautiously, "Sir?"

"What is it, Jupiter?" The merchant's face bore an expression of honest concern.

"Is there some place be willing have me sit at a table?" Calabar held out his arm before himself, demonstrating the color of his skin.

The merchant's expression reflected the fact that he was clearly surprised at the thought that anything so crass should interfere with his vision for their meal to come. "I assure you, gentle man, that my money will spend as well for your meal as for mine."

Nonetheless, Calabar could see a shadow of doubt cross the other man's face, even as he spoke. The merchant then waved his hand as though a blackfly pursued him. "In any event, we have business to transact here before we will need to deal with that question. The indigo sellers usually gather back there" – he pointed to the far corner of the pavilion – "but, of course, you have probably been here before with your old master, helping him to sell the indigo you had produced?"

Calabar shook his head, and again the merchant waved his hand to dispel the issue. "No matter, I will show you the way."

Again, Calabar had to hurry to keep up with the man, and as they moved through the crowded market, several of the buyers and sellers called out to the merchant in cheerful greeting.

"After something in particular today, Mister Cooper?"

"Can I interest you in some top-quality cordage, sir?"

"Ho, there, Henry, what are you up to with the negro – finally got yourself a serving-boy?"

The merchant whirled around at this last call, locating the speaker with a fierce glare. He put his hand on Calabar's shoulder and called back, "My associate, Jupiter Greene, happens to be a freeman and an authority on the production and assessment of the indigo, Mister Harper, and the color of his skin does not reduce that fact by one whit. I will thank you kindly to mind your manners when you address me – or him – in the future."

The plantation owner who had called out clenched his jaw, but did not answer audibly, instead fixing Calabar with a fierce glare of disapproval. Calabar avoided his eyes, following Cooper back to where the indigo farmers would be.

They stopped before a small handcart bearing a meager pile of indigo bricks, and Cooper waved him forward. The farmer who slouched beside the cart looked weary and drawn, but his eyes narrowed as Calabar approached the indigo. Addressing Cooper, he said, "Am I to take it by what you just said that you mean to have this boy judge the fitness of my product, sir?"

Cooper nodded serenely and the farmer drew himself up straight. "No, sir, that will not do. If you will take the word of a negro over my own testimony as to the high quality of my indigo, why, I do not believe that we have any business at all to conduct."

Calabar backed away, giving Cooper a small shake of his head. He had already seen enough of the bricks to note that they were indifferently formed, and he could see pale discoloration on the corner of one, a sure indication that the bricks had been left to be exposed to sunlight, to the detriment of the quality of the dye. Shampee would have kept a closer eye on them than this farmer's crew had obviously done.

Cooper caught his eye and nodded, winking. "Is that so, sir?" He raised his voice. "If there is any man here who thinks he can do a better job of picking out the top quality indigo of two bricks presented him than can my associate Jupiter, let him stand forth now."

Silence fell over the short row of indigo sellers, and the farmer before them seemed to shrink back down. "I reckon I could, if I cared to," he said, spitting into the dirt at Calabar's feet. "But there ain't no way I will set myself up to be judged by a negro, freeman or no."

Cooper nodded, a small smile crossing his mouth, though his eyes did not smile. "Your indigo has already been judged, good sir, and found lacking. Jupiter, for what reason should we decline to purchase this man's load?"

Calabar swallowed hard, feeling the intensity of the farmer's glare fixed on him. "Well, sir, the bricks be poor shape, corners knocked off, and they not be even. But they also show the sun done struck them, and they be spoilt some by it."

If Cooper had not been present, Calabar was certain that he would have received a whipping at that instant, no matter what papers he had or did not have. As it was, he felt his stomach lurch as the farmer started forward, hatred in his eyes.

"It ain't my fault that them lazy bastards I feed and take care of do such a bad job!" he yelled, his face turning red. "I tell them and I tell them, and there ain't one of them who can be bothered." Turning abruptly away from Cooper and Calabar, he reached back under his cart.

Calabar felt Cooper stiffen beside him, and then exhale and relax as the farmer drew up a rough hempen cloth and flipped it over his load, glaring at the two of them. Muttering under his breath, the farmer stooped and lifted the handles of his cart, pushing it ahead of him as he left, evidently giving up for the day on selling his low-quality indigo.

Cooper gave Calabar an approving nod, obviously pleased at having gotten the freedman's counsel. He motioned Calabar forward to the next seller, whose indigo he could see instantly was better, but not as good as he could have produced. In a whispered consultation with Cooper, they agreed that this load would do if none better could be found, but they resolved to continue looking.

They advanced through another couple of carts and tables displaying bricks of the blue dye, identifying one other potential supplier, until they reached the end of the row.

There, in the corner, he was surprised to see Jake and John standing beside a wagon stacked high with indigo bricks. John appeared to be bored, picking at his teeth with a rolled-up blade of grass, but Jake nodded in polite acknowledgement to Calabar.

Cooper strode up to Jake, shaking his hand enthusiastically.

"I found him, right where you said he'd be, and if he knows half as much about the indigo trade as you represented to me, I'll make my fortune. Of course, other matters may intrude, particularly this latest noise about a new non-importation compact, which could excite the Parliament into rash action against our ports to equal what they have done to Boston."

He seemed ready to continue in this vein for any given amount of time, but Jake's slow smile stopped him.

"Henry, we are prepared to make you a handsome bargain on this indigo, once Jupiter has given you the assurances you sought as to its quality. However, I have been told that the ship to London sails upon the tide on the morrow, and the cooper still needs a day to pack goods into barrels, so time is not your friend."

"Of course, of course. Jupiter, would you come here and kindly take measure of the load of indigo that these men have to offer?"

Calabar felt that something about this whole situation was slightly amiss, but then, what had been right since Greene had sent him away?

He said simply, "Yes, sir," and went to the back of the wagon – he recognized it as the same in which he'd ridden on that terrible day – and lifted up one of the bricks of indigo, examining its underside for any variation of its substance, and to assure himself that it had been properly cured in the sun.

Satisfied on that account, he scraped a tiny bit off the corner of the brick with his fingernail and smelled it. There was no hint of soda ash, used by some makers to settle out the dye, but at the expense of its ability to fix an even shade in cloth.

He touched his other index finger to his tongue and carefully wetted the dye, then wiped it over the tail of his tunic. The color was deep and even, and he nodded, giving an involuntary grunt of approval. Cooper had joined him at the back of the wagon, and was watching him intently.

Looking over to Cooper, he said quietly, "This be the best indigo I ever did seen. It be fetching a good price at London, I be certain."

Cooper nodded in acknowledgment and turned to Jake. He reached into his waistcoat and pulled out a coin purse, clearly heavy with coins. "Here's the price we discussed. 'Tis a good thing that I made the offer I did, before Jupiter gave such a glowing review." He winked at Jake, adding, "See to it that Greene gets his due, and make the necessary arrangements for shipment at once."

Turning back to Calabar, who stood in mute shock at the revelation that he had just handled the final product of his own work on the plantation, he said, "Shall we find someplace to sup, then, Jupiter? I feel like celebrating our new partnership."

Chapter 7

Calabar did not care for the taste of tea, finding it too much reminiscent of the medicinal concoctions that Affey sometimes made for him when he was ailing. The thought filled him with melancholy, even as Cooper urged a plate of unfamiliar, heavy food on him.

"Here, here, you must try the ham," the merchant said, pushing a slab of strangely pink, heavily fat-encircled meat onto Calabar's plate. Tucking into an even bigger slab on his own plate, Cooper said, past a mouthful of meat, "It's from Virginia, although" – he leaned in as though confiding a great secret – "I do believe that they make a finer ham in these parts, when they can find a suitable hog what has been fattened up on ground nuts, and then set it up to cure for half a year or better, but the folk here and in Virginia like to put on airs and say that only the genuine article brought in from there will do."

Sitting back, Cooper motioned to the ham on Calabar's plate with his knife, raising his eyebrows and urging the other man to try it. Calabar took up his own knife and fork – Cooper had insisted that he use them, no matter how clumsy the tools felt in his hands – and managed to butcher a reasonably sized morsel of the meat from the slab.

He put it in his mouth and felt as though his senses were being assailed, as the intense saltiness of the food competed with its unfamiliar and overwhelming array of flavors. The texture was strange to him as well, firmer and more uniform than the rare treat of boiled chicken meat he was accustomed to. He struggled to keep the surprise he was feeling from showing through on his face, as Cooper watched him avidly, clearly expecting the freeman to exclaim in pure delight at the experience of trying this ham for the first time.

Calabar managed to finish chewing and swallowed it, then grabbed the tea, which had, thankfully, cooled enough that it did not scald his throat as he drank it down to reduce the cacophony of flavors to something that he could bear. Of course, the tea itself made his mouth feel as though it were strangely dry, particularly after the saltiness of the ham.

As Calabar's face reflected the overwhelming strangeness that he was experiencing in trying out these new foods, Cooper sat back, crossing his arms over his chest and frowning slightly. "Didn't care for it much, I take it," the merchant said, as a statement of fact, rather than as a question.

Calabar made a face reflecting his ambivalence, as he began to be able to actually sort out and start to decide whether he liked it at all or not. "No, sir, it be not so at all. I never been eating so well, it is."

His mouth working to pick meat from between his teeth, he added, "It be not at all yams and chicken, and not beans and hominy."

Cooper nodded, mollified. "Yes, of course, I should have thought of that. You are accustomed to a pretty plain diet, and I set before you food that is rich even to my palate. Perhaps the tavern keeper can be persuaded to find something more to your liking?"

Calabar felt his face go hot in shame at his own simplicity, and he said hastily, "No, sir, I be certain that I will be liking this just fine." To emphasize the point, he cut off another piece of the ham and put it into his mouth.

It was still overwhelming, but at least this time he was braced for it. He smiled at his benefactor, and hoped that his gratitude to the trader was evident. As he chewed, he pondered the turn of fate that had brought him to share this meal with Cooper. He found that he had to make a conscious effort to avoid thinking of the man as "Master" Cooper – after all, they were both free men, neither beholden to the other beyond their business transaction.

Cooper slurped at his tea, evidently lost in his own thoughts. As Calabar ventured another sliver of ham, Cooper said slowly, "Jupiter, we did not previously discuss the terms of our partnership, and it seems reasonable that we come to an agreement that is to your satisfaction and mine."

He patted his waistcoat, and Calabar could hear the clink of money within. "I expect to make a pretty profit on that load of indigo. With your particular expertise in describing its quality to the factor at the docks, I should be able to make over again the amount that I paid for it."

His eyes narrowed slightly and he looked closely at Calabar. "Do you know the value of money at all, or has your prior state left you innocent of it?"

Calabar shook his head, feeling his cheeks warm slightly. "No, sir, I never been have money, for any reason."

Cooper nodded and sat back in his chair. "You are fortunate, then, to have come into the company of someone like myself, for I have a keen understanding of the value of a guinea, but am not so grasping as to lead you astray by persuading you that the value of your knowledge was but a handful of half-crowns."

Reaching into his waistcoat, he produced the coin purse and opened it, fishing about within it for a moment. He triumphantly laid a large coin made of a shiny yellowish metal onto the table in front of him, bearing an image of a dour-looking man with a weak chin. It made a dull clunk on the wood, and Cooper said, "This is the guinea, worth a pound and a shilling."

His face taking on a shrewd expression, he looked Calabar over and pronounced, "Were you still in a condition of servitude, you would likely sell for about forty guineas, more if the buyer had some sense of your peculiar skills, less if he were valuing you for mere field labor."

Calabar felt his blood run cold at the frank assessment of his price as a piece of property, and it was in that moment that he realized that he was, indeed, no longer merely property. Cooper, heedless of the former slave's epiphany, pressed on with his lesson. "The price I paid for the indigo this afternoon was dear – over two hundred guineas – but I expect to sell it at the docks within the fortnight for three hundred fifty or better."

Setting a second coin, larger and made of a grey metal, beside the first, he said, "This is a crown. It is not so common as the half-crown, which I'll show you in a moment, but 'tis important for you to know that four of these are worth a pound sterling." Feigning deep interest, Calabar peered closely at the coin, noting that the face on it appeared to be that of a different man, and that it was much more worn than the first coin.

He nodded and sat back, and Cooper laid down a third coin. It looked like a smaller version of the crown, featuring the face of what appeared to be the same man, and almost as grey and worn as the larger coin. "This is the half-crown, worth two shillings and sixpence. Two of these are worth as much as a crown. I'll pay for our meal with these two" – he indicated the last ones he'd set out – "though I'll ordinarily eat less fine. Do you understand so far?"

Calabar nodded, mentally working out the relationships in the values of these coins, and adding up how many of them his life might have been purchased for. A great bulging purse full of these would have been required to purchase him, before he was freed. Somehow that was more satisfying than the mere double handful of guineas Cooper had referred to, but he was still coming to grips with the fact that he might have been – had been, as a child – exchanged for a handful of coins, far smaller than had purchased the cartload of fine indigo.

Cooper grinned, unaware of the bitter thoughts that roiled the other man's mind. "Now things get more complicated." He laid down a fourth coin, which was less grey and shinier, while smaller yet, and bearing the same weak-chinned man's image. "A shilling. Five of these make a crown, twenty to the pound."

Another grey coin joined the bewildering assortment. "Sixpence; two to the shilling, and a sixpence will get you a loaf of bread and a mug of small beer most anyplace in the colony." He scattered a handful of smaller coins across the table, pointing to them in turn. "Threepence, a penny, and a ha-penny. You'll most likely see these in the purchase of your news-papers, or to make change." Calabar was vaguely familiar with the concept of a news-paper, but could scarcely imagine purchasing one himself.

Cooper shrugged. "Mostly, they collect at the bottom of your purse, and you must remember to spend them, lest they drag you to the ground. Though they are small, they seem to multiply like rats, in my purse at least."

The lesson concluded, Cooper swept all but the crown and half-crown coins off the edge of the table into his hand and dropped them into his purse, which he then put back away.

"Now, in the ordinary course of matters, I would have bought the indigo with script – paper issued by a bank or even the Crown, promising that it could be exchanged for a like amount of coin – but by paying in specie, I was able to shave a few guineas more off the price I needed to offer. Gold always spends, no matter what the rowdy fellows in Boston or Charles-Town might get up to." He smiled at his own wit and took another sip of his tea.

Sitting back, his expression now turned more serious and shrewd. "If I clear one hundred and fifty guineas on the sale of that indigo, I would consider that at least a quarter of that profit is due to the particular knowledge that your participation in the transaction contributes. Of course, I cannot simply grant you all of that difference, else the advantage to me of our partnership becomes the same as if I had simply undertaken the exercise without the advantage of your wisdom."

Chewing his lip for a moment and staring into space, he finally asked, "Would you consider that a one-eighth share of the profit, net of costs, would be a fair division of the spoils?"

Calabar's brow beetled as he struggled to understand what was being asked. It sounded as though the merchant were offering to give him a substantial share of money, over and above the meal, but he did not trust to believe that such largesse could be his lot.

"Please, sir, I be not understanding."

Cooper nodded and a small smile played across his face. "Of

course, I should not have expected that you could figure what such a share might be worth, when you have only just been offered the first opportunity to learn what the money itself is."

Gesturing with his head toward the stairs, he asked Jupiter, "How much are you paying for a room here? As much as a shilling, I'll wager, as they include ordinary meals?"

Jupiter felt his face go hot as he answered slowly, "I been not staying in a room, sir." Indeed, sleeping rough in the alleyway behind the inn had been a chancy option, but the only one he'd yet found. There weren't that many rats to compete with for discarded crusts of bread, and the owners of the surrounding buildings had not yet ejected him.

Cooper waved a dismissive hand. "No matter; I shall see to it tonight, and once the indigo sells, you should have money sufficient to stay here for a year, should you so desire. If I should sell the load for three hundred fifty, as I hope, every eighth guinea of the one hundred fifty we clear from the transaction would be yours."

Jupiter tried to work out what his share of such a sum would be, and was stunned into disbelief at the answers he was reaching. For the price of an afternoon's walking and answering simple questions, he might live in the luxury of being out of the weather, with food set before him every day, for an entire year? He was certain that he must have misunderstood what Cooper was saying.

"Please, sir, a year? For saying that an indigo was bad and another better, enough to stay tavern for a whole year?"

Cooper guffawed. "No, Jupiter – you will have earned a year of bed and beans for having spent many years learning to know which indigo to say was bad, and which was better. I or anyone could merely say the words, but you are the one unbiased person I know of in this city who could, at a glance, know which load about which to say them."

Cooper blinked hard and thought for a moment. "Let me set it before you this way: Without I should have had your advice, I might have suspected that the indigo we purchased was of good quality. With your advice, however, I know that it is of superior grade, and should command a premium price at the docks. Knowing that, I can ask the top guinea for it, and I will make much more money than I would have absent your knowledge."

Seeing that Jupiter's face still bore a confused frown, he added, "As I said before, I would credit your knowledge with about a quarter of the profit I expect to make – to put it differently, I should have made only three-quarters of the profit I expect to, had I not asked your advice."

Jupiter nodded, believing that he understood at least partially. A wild thought then struck him, and he asked, his heart beginning to hammer in his chest, "Please, sir, if we buy, sell more indigo, I earn enough guineas to buy my wife and daughter from Master Greene?"

Cooper's head turned sharply to look at Jupiter, an understanding of his own dawning on his face. He said thoughtfully, "That might be possible, Jupiter, though I can make no assurances as to your old master's price for them, nor his willingness to sell them out of bondage at all."

He was surprised to see Jupiter's eyes brimming with unshed tears as the other man nodded mutely. Placing his hands atop Jupiter's, he added, "However, that is a fine goal to set, and I'll do what I can to help you meet it."

Chapter 8

Calabar awoke with a start, aware that he was somehow not where he belonged. Rather than the comforting solidity of the ground beneath his bedding, he was suspended over open air, and the sensation was disconcerting.

After a moment of looking about the room in which he awoke disoriented, he remembered that this was his room, that Cooper had smoothed things over with the tavern keeper the prior evening when that worthy had expressed reservations about letting a freed slave sleep under his roof. The matter had been settled by his new business partner offering to pay for a month in advance, placing a guinea into the tavern keeper's hand.

Apparently, gold was an effective counter to whatever reservations the tavern keeper held, and the man had led Jupiter to this room, saying as he departed, "So long as you keep to yourself and don't try to put on airs amongst your betters, there'll be no trouble. I'm putting you in your own room so as to keep it quiet that I've let a room to a negro." The man had looked sharply at Jupiter, adding, "You be sure to tell that Mister Cooper what I done for you."

Jupiter had scowled behind the tavern keeper's back, but had kept his tongue, knowing that to do otherwise was to put himself back out in the alleyway – and this time, he suspected that the tavern keeper would be a more determined foe than the rats.

He had long practice in keeping his thoughts to himself, though it rankled more after being treated like a real person by Cooper all day.

Shaking his head at the memory, Calabar swung his legs over the side of the bed and stretched, wincing. He almost thought that the alley had been more comfortable than this bed, at least so far as sleeping was concerned. Perhaps, he thought, he might try sleeping on the floor that evening, to learn whether it was any more comfortable.

Now, though, there was bread and a cider waiting for him downstairs, and he found that even without having spent the prior day at hard labor, he was still quite hungry. He pulled his rough trousers on over his shirt and opened the door to his room, grunting at finding a full plate and mug on the floor outside. Obviously, the tavern keeper intended to keep him out of sight . . . although it seemed unlikely to Calabar that that could last for long.

He shrugged, retrieved his breakfast, and sat down to eat on the plain wooden chair that sat beside his bed. In addition to the bread that he'd anticipated – a whole loaf all to himself, and still warm from the ovens! – there was a wedge of cheese, which Calabar sniffed curiously and then nibbled at. It wasn't bad when followed by a sip of cider, and a bite of bread made it even more palatable.

He was nearly finished with the cheese and halfway through the loaf of bread when there was a knock at the door. He set the plate down on his bed and approached the door, standing by the handle suspiciously.

"Who be there?"

"It's me, Jupiter, Mister Cooper. May I enter?"

Calabar opened the door wide, a smile stealing over his face. "Mister Cooper, I be glad see you!"

"And I am glad to see you as well, Jupiter. I thought that you might enjoy coming with me down to the docks to see how the negotiation for the indigo proceeds, and to vouch for its quality, should the question arise." He looked Calabar over and frowned at the other man's rough, grey clothing and bare feet.

"First, though, I think it might help my cause should we visit the milliner, the tailor and the shoemaker. I presume that you do not object to spending some of your share in advance to be clothed and shod properly?"

Calabar blinked hard at the thought, remembering his lost shoes, and how fine and proud he felt wearing them. He nodded slowly.

Cooper nodded in reply, adding, "We should be able to get you a proper pair of breeches to replace those, as well as shoes, straight away, and a decent shirt and waistcoat made within a few days. You ought have a hat as well, though I would advise you against a wig, as hot as the summer is here."

"Oh, I have my hat," Calabar said, turning back to the bed to pick up his pockets, which he tied around his waist and then fished into, producing a knitted cap. He jammed it onto his head and grinned. "See?"

Cooper visibly contained his reaction, and reached under his arm to tap the hat he had tucked there. "Perhaps more along these lines?"

Calabar grinned again, saying, "I knowed what you meant. Just having fun." He frowned and added, "Do I need all that?"

"Oh yes, and stockings and a cravat, too. I think we can

get away without a greatcoat for you, at least so long as it does not rain, but you should dress as a freeman, and not as a slave, lest someone mistake you for a runaway."

Calabar felt his face flush, and he reached into his pocket again. Brandishing the letter that Master Greene had grudgingly scratched out, he said, "Have proof I am free here, no man can slave me."

Cooper nodded, his expression serious. "I agree, my friend, but it is not decent to expect to be challenged for a slip of paper at every turn, simply to prove that you have the right to walk on the street unmolested. Clothing will save you from ever needing to display your freedom on a paper again."

Calabar considered this briefly. "Then I have clothes, keep paper put away safe." He gathered the bread from his plate and stuffed the last bit of cheese in his mouth, chasing it with the final swallow of cider. "I be ready."

Chapter 9

The tailor took Calabar's measurements silently, under the watchful eye of Mister Cooper. He was, perhaps, less gentle than he might have been with Mister Cooper himself, his measuring-tape binding and his fingertips jabbing as he noted one dimension after another in spidery-looking handwriting upon a small ledger on the table.

He kept glancing up at Calabar's face, as though in disbelief that he was standing and kneeling before a former slave towering above him on his measuring bench, purchasing his goods just as any other customer might do.

At least he had agreed to serve the freedman. The first tailor they had visited had pursed his lips as they entered, saying brusquely, "Your boy can wait outside whilst I attend to you."

Cooper had looked startled, and had then scowled, answering, "My associate is a freedman and your customer, sir, unless you should prefer that we spend his money elsewhere." The man had scowled and silently shook his head, hooking his thumb toward the door.

Cooper, his face flushed, had seemed ready to spit out an insult, but had contained himself, turning on his heel and leaving, Calabar following even more eagerly than he had entered.

Once they were out of earshot, the merchant had started mumbling a steady stream of imprecations under his breath, only calming as they approached another tailor's shop. Calabar was surprised into silence to hear one white man speak about another in such terms, using words he had only ever before heard applied to field slaves by particularly brutal foremen, words that usually presaged a whipping.

As they had approached the second tailor's shop, Cooper had said, "Wait here for a moment, while I check to see if this man is less of a brute than the last." He'd ducked inside while Calabar stood, nervous as always when in public alone, and had emerged to wave the freedman inside the shop with him.

Calabar stood mute as the merchant and the tailor bargained in rapid fire over the price of pants, shirts, and the other clothing he needed. It seemed to him as though the tailor's heart was not in the negotiation, though, as the man kept glancing nervously over to him and then toward the street, as though afraid that the mere presence of a black man in his premises would drive off his customers.

"Two pair of breeches enough, Jupiter?" Cooper's sudden question jarred Calabar out of his bitter recollections as the tailor scratched down the final details of his measurements. The two men looked at him expectantly, and Calabar almost chuckled aloud at the specter of white men looking up to him, waiting with anticipation for his pleasure.

The moment passed and he nodded. "Two pair be plenty." It was more pairs of breeches than he'd owned before at least, and he was quite certain that they would be far better than the rough slave trousers, sewn together though they were with care by Affey. The thought gave him a pang of guilt and sadness, which he suppressed quickly. There would be plenty of time to ponder his regrets and sorrows in the privacy of his room that night.

The tailor turned away, his lips pursed tightly. Cooper called after him, "The same price for both, of course. Were it more pairs, I might argue for a discount, owing to the savings in your time of being able to cut them all to the same measurements, but I cannot see pushing our luck any further." The tailor stopped and nodded sharply before continuing to his counter to work up the figures for the freedman's outfitting.

Turning back to Calabar, Cooper continued, "I recommend at least three shirts and at least as many pairs of stockings, but I make do with just the one waistcoat and, unless you are a slob at the table, a single cravat should likewise do."

"I be a careful eater, Mister Cooper." Calabar smiled quickly, and Cooper nodded to the tailor, who scowled again and continued his figuring.

Cooper gave the tailor an ingratiating smile as Calabar stepped down from the stool. "Can you recommend a reputable milliner as well? My associate will, of course, require a hat, and if you know someone who can make a decent pair of shoes, suitable for life in town, we would likewise be much obliged to you."

The tailor snorted and replied, "Them what will serve his lot are few in this town, but you might try Barstowe's, under his sign four doors down, for the shoes, and old man Allbright around the corner can't much afford to turn away any business, so I'd reckon that he'd make this fellow a hat."

He pushed the bill across the counter to Cooper, who shook his head and pointed toward Calabar with a small motion of just his index finger. The tailor's eyebrows rose and he retorted, disbelieving, "He reads?"

"No, sir," Cooper said. "But he pays his own way, like any

other man of the colony. If you would be so kind as to inform him what the total is, I will warrant that his purse is good for it."

The tailor named a figure and Cooper's eyes narrowed slightly. "If you would like, Jupiter, I can check the man's figures." The tailor scowled more deeply and pulled the paper back, scratching out the total with a quick motion and writing down a new number, which he read off to Calabar, as Cooper looked on with a frown of reproval.

Calabar fumbled in his pockets, trying to figure out the right coins to give the tailor, and Cooper said, "Our friend here will be glad to make change for you, should you want to just lay down a couple of guineas." He smiled tightly at the tailor, an expression that did not reach his suddenly hard eyes. "I am certain that he will count it out most carefully for you."

Calabar felt a flash of gratitude yet again toward the merchant, and he fished out the two heavy gold coins, putting them down on the counter and smiling inwardly at the satisfying ring of metal on wood. The tailor counted out his change with exaggerated care, and Cooper nodded at him in acknowledgment.

"Thank you, sir," said Calabar, gathering up the sparse handful of coins and dropping them into his pocket with the remainder of the money that Cooper had given him that morning – "An advance on your earnings, not a loan, never a loan" – and the two men left the shop, emerging to blink at the bright sunlight without.

As soon as they were out of earshot, Cooper leaned over toward Calabar and said quietly, "I'd check those clothes over closely when we return to receive delivery of them." He frowned to himself. "I'll ask an associate of mine to keep an eye on him, too, that he keeps at the work steadily until it is done, so that you may be properly dressed as quickly as possible."

The cobbler was perfectly happy to serve them, in a welcome contrast to the tailors, and Calabar walked out carrying a pair of shoes equipped with plain buckles, having been instructed in their use by Cooper. He would have worn them, but both the shoemaker and the merchant exclaimed that he must wait until he had stockings, to preserve the leather.

The milliner, an old man with one eye covered with a roughly tied cloth, was downright delighted to hear the tale of Calabar's liberation from servitude. "Slavery's a foul stain on these colonies," he said, the strong smell of rum on his breath at odds with his steady gaze and careful hands, as he tried one cocked hat and then another on Calabar's head. "You mark my words, the day will come when we will be judged and found sorely wanting on the balance of heaven itself."

He nodded to himself, satisfied with the fit of the third hat he put on Calabar. "You'll not be wearing a wig, I wager?"

Calabar shook his head, still pondering the strangeness of a man who had never served in bondage expressing such strong opposition to the institution. "Good," said the milliner. "Silly affectation, you ask me, and an invitation to vermin." He glanced over at Cooper. "Begging your pardon, sir, if you like a wig."

Cooper raised a hand and smiled. "You'll find no argument from me," he said, adding, "This climate is too stifling for them to be a practicality, in any case."

The milliner gave a quick bark of laughter. "But those dandies who fancy themselves proper macaronis will always put style well in front of the practical considerations, now won't they, even as they drop in the summer sun."

He turned back to Calabar. "Should you like a glass to examine how the hat sets on you, friend, or will you accept the word of those who behold you?"

Calabar swallowed suddenly. Though he'd caught glimpses of himself in puddles and windows on occasion, he'd never had the luxury of examining himself in a proper looking glass. "Please, sir, I be liking a glass. I never been buying a hat before."

The old man smiled broadly. "Of course, friend, and a grand occasion it should be, too." He pulled a small mirror of polished metal out from under his counter, handing it to the freedman.

Calabar held it up, quickly figuring out how to angle it so that he could examine the hat – and his own face. Sad eyes looked out at him from a somber face, under the point of a plain, but functional, cocked hat.

He thought that he looked thinner than he had expected, and was surprised to see a touch of grey in his sideburns. His beard was shot through with silvery hairs as well, and seeing it grown out gave him another pang – Affey had kept his face shaved, and he had no idea how he was to maintain it without a wife to help him.

Solemnly, he handed the glass back to the milliner, touched his hand to the brim of the hat and asked, "How much do I pay?"

The milliner stashed the looking glass back under his counter and pulled at his lower lip thoughtfully. Finally he asked, "How long were you a slave, friend?"

Puzzled, Calabar answered, "I been slave since I been a boy."

The old man nodded and scratched absently at the edge of the cloth covering his eye. Speaking slowly and deliberately, he said, "As I figure it, then, you have been robbed of better than a score of years of your life. Who am I to demand anything more from you for a mere hat?"

He laced his hands together and pressed them to the countertop and fixed Calabar's eyes with a fierce gaze from his own one good eye. "I'll take no money from you for the hat, friend, only your word that you will never fall into the habit of accepting the vile concept that one man may justly claim ownership of another."

Calabar swallowed hard and nodded, fighting back sudden tears that threatened to spill down his face. When he could trust his ability to speak without his voice breaking, he said, "Thank you, sir. I be in your debt." As the other man began to object, he added, bringing his hand to his breast, "Not for hat. For heart."

The old milliner nodded. "You are welcome, friend, and I give you the joy of your liberty. Anyone who might ask where you came to acquire such a fine hat, you can tell them that it was a gift from Thomas Allbright, master milliner."

Calabar said, "I will, Mister Allbright." He bowed his head in gratitude and turned to leave. He was surprised to find Mister Cooper's eyes bright with nascent tears as well. The merchant bowed respectfully to the milliner, and they took their leave of his shop.

The merchant drew out his snuffbox as they returned to the street and applied snuff to his nostrils, blowing his nose noisily afterward. "Shall we sup, before we go down to the docks to make our fortune?"

Calabar touched the brim of his new hat, and motioned for Cooper to lead the way. Although the merchant said nothing outward about the milliner's gesture of generosity, he was uncharacteristically quiet for the remainder of the way back to the tavern, leaving Calabar to ponder the morning's events in the peace and solitude of his own thoughts.

Chapter 10

Calabar's impression of the docks was still that they were smelly, noisy, and dangerous. Worse to his nose even than the familiar stench of indigo working in its vats was the all-pervading odor of fish, overworked laborers moving cargo about, and other things better left unexamined.

As they walked along the quay, Calabar was surprised to see a woman in tattered clothes having a loud and energetic argument with an unsavory-looking man, a laborer by the manner of his dress. He could not make out what they were saying to one another, but it was clear from the hoarseness of her voice that they had been at it for some time.

Cooper and Calabar were just getting close enough to hear a few words when the workman gave out a guttural shout, yelling quite distinctly, "Oh, no you don't, Angela!" Calabar gasped to see that the woman had reached down into her boot and now brandished a wicked-looking knife in her hand. Cooper stopped and put out his arm before Calabar, as though to restrain him from interfering.

Two men lounging in the open door of a warehouse nudged each other, and Calabar could swear that he heard them laying odds with one another over the outcome of the fight. Cooper shot the pair an angry glare, and they faded back into the building, although Calabar could still hear their chuckles.

The woman swung her knife wildly in the air, and as the breeze shifted, Calabar caught a whiff of stale rum or ale from the pair, and he noticed then that both of the fighters were so intoxicated that they were clearly having trouble keeping their feet.

The woman let out a wordless shriek and ran at the man, the knife held before her like a skewer. He ducked aside at the last moment, and she stumbled past him and disappeared over the edge of the dock, making a muffled-sounding splash in the murky water of the harbor.

Both Cooper and Calabar ran forward then, as the target of the woman's attack shuffled over to the side of the dock, blinking slowly down into the water. As Cooper arrived at his side, the drunkard called out plaintively into the water, "Angela?"

Calabar reached the side of the dock just as the woman surfaced, still waving the knife in the air in the general direction of the man, but otherwise appearing to make little effort to either save herself or even stay afloat. After a long moment, she sank back beneath the filthy water, her upraised blade the last thing to disappear into the murk.

The drunkard cried out again and, although Cooper attempted to restrain him, he lurched toward the edge of the dock as well, brushing the merchant's arm aside. He tripped at the edge and, his arms flailing like a windmill, he went over the side in a completely uncontrolled fall. The water closed over him almost without a splash, and he never even surfaced. Only a large bubble, surfacing after a few moments, betrayed that anything had taken place at the water's edge.

Cooper looked back at Calabar, both of them in shock at the double tragedy they had just witnessed. Cooper shook his head in disbelief, finally finding words. "I have never seen such a thing in all my time along these docks. I . . . I don't know what we ought do."

Just then, one of the men jogged out of the nearby warehouse, stopping at the edge of the water and staring down, dumbfounded. "They done both gone in?"

"Yes," Cooper confirmed. "You know them?"

"Why, surely. That had been Old Jerry and his woman, Angela. We always did think that they'd wind up one of them killin' the other, but I would never have thought that they'd both do each other in! Mean pair of drunks, they is, always lurking about and asking for tuppence for an ale, or sixpence for a meal. Couple of us sometimes done took pity and flipped them a coin, but I can't guess that they'll be missed."

Cooper said gravely, "I don't expect that it is worth the time of the constabulary to attempt their rescue, then."

The warehouse man shook his head violently. "No, sir. The sheriff done told them already to make for some other place, and I'll be thrice cursed if I want to bring him down here to come poking around. Beggin' your pardon, but there be some things what one don't want the law paying too close a mind to, if you know what I mean."

He glanced significantly toward his warehouse, and Cooper leaned over to say quietly to Calabar, "I do believe that he means smuggling." Calabar's eyebrows went up, but he did not otherwise react outwardly. More loudly, Cooper said to the man, "I was just telling my associate that I think it best if we were on our way to our own business."

The man nodded, peering over the edge again. He

commented, "I won't miss them skulking about, always trying our locks after dark and so forth." Looking back up to Cooper, he added quickly, "It ain't that I wish ill to any man – or woman – but the loss of these two won't bother none but the rats what had hoped to gnaw their bones."

Calabar shuddered. Cooper made a sour face and then led the freedman down the quay without further comment. The two of them walked briskly, trying to shake off the melancholy that had settled over them both. The merchant perked up as they approached a row of immense warehouses, the largest on the docks, and Calabar did his best to do likewise, at least outwardly.

Cooper led him to a warehouse filled with seemingly endless stacks of barrels, each marked with cryptic symbols of one variety or another. Some were letters – although Calabar was ignorant of their meaning, he'd seen them often enough on signs and printed pages to know what they were – but others were plain lines, circles drawn about groups of letters, or even simple drawings. They might have been the scribblings of children, but for the fact that they appeared with utter regularity on barrel after barrel.

A tall, imposing man stood inside the door of the warehouse, surrounded by a few others, and Calabar noted with surprise and curiosity that he had a large, wildly colored bird perched upon his shoulder. What was more, he seemed to be including the bird in his conversations with the other men, cocking his head to listen to its squawks and croaks.

Calabar was even more surprised to realize that the bird's cries were actually comprehensible as speech, as they drew near enough to hear them more clearly. Cooper put a hand on Calabar's arm to indicate that they should stop and observe from a decent distance, whispering, "That's Captain Brand, and it will be our turn to treat with him shortly."

The captain turned to his companion, asking, "What say ye, Toby? Be he offering a fair price on the goods?"

The bird tilted its head a few times jerkily, blinking in apparent thought before answering, "Nay, nay, nay. He's a cheat, a liar, a cheat." The tall man's eyebrows went up as he made a show of considering the bird's counsel before he turned back to one of the men with whom he appeared to be negotiating.

"Be the bird a teller of the truth then, Mister Jones? I warn you, Toby has never failed me before."

The shorter man swallowed hard and stammered, "I – I – I thought that the tobacco was of top quality, but if you think otherwise, I can withdraw the bill of sale and offer it elsewhere."

The tall man's eyebrows rose even further, disappearing entirely under the wide brim of his sailor's hat. "Oh, so ye reckon ye can cheat some other honest man out of his gold? Nay, sir, I think I will buy your tobacco, but I'll give you no more than twenty quid for each of them light-packed hogsheads. Thirty be outright robbery, and ye know it well."

The smaller man drew himself up stiffly and fixed the captain with a fierce gaze, his voice steeling as much as his spine. "Those hogsheads measure up exactly as they are claimed, good sir. I am of a mind to demand satisfaction for your insult!"

The captain grinned widely and put his hands on his hips, drawing back the sides of his greatcoat to reveal an ornate pistol on one side and a wicked, curved sword on the other. "Are ye, now?" He shook his head theatrically. "I meant no insult by it, but if you demand satisfaction, I would advise you to wind up your earthly affairs first." The tobacco seller again swallowed visibly, his eyes tracing the length of the sword.

The captain crossed his arms over his chest, letting his coat close back over his weapons. "I'll tell ye what, sir. I'll take your word as good that the barrels are honest packed. There's so much of the weed in the markets this year, though, that I cannot be sure of finding a good market in London-town. Will ye take adequate satisfaction in an offer of twenty-four each?"

The seller also crossed his arms over his chest, his eyes narrowed and still obviously biting back rage. He spat out, "Twenty-seven."

Without hesitation, the captain barked back, "Twenty-five four."

The seller reached out reluctantly to shake the captain's hand, and the multicolored bird bobbed up and down excitedly on the tall man's shoulder, crying out raucously, "A deal, a deal, a deal!"

The onlookers dispersed, and Captain Brand spotted Cooper and Calabar, calling out with a broad smile, "Mister Cooper, 'tis a pleasure to see you again, sir. And your companion, be he a Moor or a servant?"

Cooper strode forward, clasping the captain's offered hand cheerfully. "Neither, Captain. He is a freedman, late of the indigo production, and my partner in our current enterprise."

The captain's face registered a moment of surprise, and then he turned his full attention to Calabar. Under the man's piercing gaze, Calabar felt as though he were laid bare in both body and soul, the captain's eyes a physical force as they roved over his face and limbs. He felt acutely self-conscious of the contrast between the rough clothing he still wore while they awaited the tailor's work, and the hat perched on his head like a shield against the judgement of the world.

After an eternal moment, the captain nodded, turning back to Cooper. "I suppose ye'll be telling me that his knowledge of the indigo is superior, and that he can vouch for the quality of your offering?"

Cooper's face paled slightly, but he did not outwardly react otherwise, only saying quietly, "Just so, sir. His late master's plantation has long been known as a producer of an indigo of exceedingly high quality. Jupiter, here, was the chief cause of that reputation, and when I learned that he had gained his freedom, I immediately sought out his counsel, so as to be able to offer you the best that the market has available this season."

The captain nodded again. "A wise move, but I expect that means that ye'll be asking a premium price, then?"

Cooper bowed graciously in answer. "It will be well worth your while, Captain."

The captain took a deep breath, his chest swelling visibly, as the bird on his shoulder shifted to keep its balance. "All right, then, Mister Cooper. What'll ye be asking for the lot of it?"

Cooper smiled and said, "The latest word I have of the markets in London is that superior indigo such as this is worth no less than seven shillings to the pound at the dock; I have loaded into barrels exactly one thousand, three hundred and fifty-nine pounds in clean, fresh bricks. I think it fair to ask four hundred seventy-five quid, cash on the barrel."

The captain reared back and let out a roar of laughter, the bird joining in with a cacophony of caws and jeers of its own. When his mirth had subsided somewhat, the captain said, "The source ye have relied upon is as crooked as that tobacco-man. I've paid no more than four shillings for the best indigo I've ever laid eyes upon, and at that, I had to make some sharp deals in London to avoid having to dress me whole crew in blue for a year, just to find some use for the stuff."

Cooper gave no quarter, retorting sharply, "What, was that five years ago, then? I know you to be a close observer of politics, so you may have noticed that there are wholly new risks to the trade since then?" He gave a sly smile. "Furthermore, I have heard word from England that indigo blue is back in fashion on the high streets, and demand is keen for the best quality. I like you, though, so I'd be willing to let you have it for six and a half per pound."

The captain smiled again, the merriment reaching his eyes as he clearly enjoyed the back-and-forth of the negotiation. Calabar let his breath out for the first time since the start of the conversation. "Five'd still be more than I've ever spent on the indigo, Cooper."

"Six and four pence would be the fairest price you'll see this side of the Atlantic, Captain."

"Six might be my ruin." The bird chose this moment to join in, echoing, "Ruin, ruin, ruin!"

"Six and tuppence will make your fortune."

The captain's hand shot out to seal the bargain, and Cooper shook it heartily, as the bird again punctuated the moment with its cry, "A deal, a deal, an excellent deal!"

Chapter II

"A toast, Jupiter!" Cooper raised his cup, his face already florid and his eyes beginning to lose coordination. Calabar's glass held only cider – the tavern keeper wasn't sure whether it was legal to sell rum to a freedman, and refused to chance it – and the partners were obliged to have a seat in the back corner, where they were less prominent. Calabar was happy enough to set aside these petty injustices after their triumph on the docks, though, and cheerfully raised his tankard to meet Cooper's cup.

"To superior market knowledge, and to the benefits one may gain by acquiring the same!" Calabar nodded agreeably, though he did not understand what exactly Cooper was talking about. What he did understand was the double fistful of guineas and small assortment of the lesser coins that Cooper had handed over to him after exchanging the captain's warrant for specie.

Cooper had gone over the figures in painstaking detail, explaining his calculations and showing where he was crediting the advance he'd given to Calabar against his share, then accounting for the amount he swept into a small leather purse for the freedman, down to the last ha'penny. Calabar, though he pretended to attend the merchant's figures closely, had no idea what the scratchings the man laid upon the page meant, as numbers were as far outside his knowledge as were letters.

But, with a purse full of coins, he reckoned any man could learn what he needed to in order to get ahead. For the first time that he could remember, his future lay like an open road before him, beckoning him to step forward eagerly. No more the daily drudge in the fields and vats; no more the uncertainty of his situation changing at his owner's whim; no more the dread of what the sunrise might bring.

In their place, clearly seen, were a reunion with Affey and Fantee, liberation for all of them, establishment in some position of responsibility and reliable income, and the potential for seeing Fantee grow up free in a world that rarely opened its doors to their kind. Despite the optimism of his mood, the thought of Affey and Fantee, still suffering the uncertainty and fear of their condition of servitude gave him a pang, and he closed his eyes for a moment to steady himself.

When he opened them, he found that there was a man sitting at a table near the door, staring at him with cold eyes. It took Calabar a moment to place him, and then he remembered that this was the tailor who had refused to suffer him to so much as stand in his shop, much less purchase his offerings. The man looked away after a moment, drained his cup and left, a small coin ringing on the table behind him.

Calabar did not know what the man's actions portended, but he doubted that it could be anything good. His fears were realized in a few minutes when the tailor returned in the company of another man. They approached the table where Calabar sat, and Cooper now slumped, the drink having gotten the better of him.

The man whom the tailor had apparently summoned nodded to Calabar, his expression neutral but his eyes narrowed in suspicion. "I trust that you are having a pleasant evening, friend," he said, touching the brim of his hat. "I am told that you are a freedman; may I see your papers?"

Calabar fumbled in his pocket for the folded evidence of his freedom, feeling a great flapping chill in his chest. As he pulled it out, the leathern purse that Cooper had gifted to him fell with a heavy clink of coins to the floor. He bent to retrieve it, and the stranger's foot swept it out of reach.

Desperately, Calabar looked up to the man. "Please, sir, that be mine, earned today."

The other man said nothing, but extended his hand for the papers, which Calabar handed over with a trembling hand. The tailor snorted behind him, muttering, "Probably stole it from his foolish and drunken friend."

The stranger shot the tailor a withering look, and turned his attention to Calabar's papers. Nodding, he said, "This says that you were set free just past a fortnight ago. You are familiar with the laws of this colony regarding freedmen, I hope?"

Calabar shook his head, mutely terrified. The stranger nodded, passing Calabar back the paper that represented his freedom. "As the sheriff of this county, it's my duty to acquaint you with the details, should you need, but the most important one for you to know is that you are bound to leave the borders of this colony not later than one year after you have become a free man; six months, were you dismissed from service for reason other than exceptional merit. Since I do not see anything in your manumission to support a claim of meritorious service, I am inclined to believe that you have six months. If you fail to leave, you may be seized by the Crown and sold back into service."

He pushed the purse back over to where Calabar could reach it, his expression softening by a degree. "You are permitted to work in whatever employment you may find, but are admonished that you must not carry debt to any man." He turned back to the tailor. "Are you satisfied, sir, as to the verity of the account you were given?"

The tailor looked disgusted at the turn of events, but nodded reluctantly. "I won't be doing any business with the likes of him, though." He tossed his head in Calabar's direction.

"Of course not," said the sheriff smoothly, his eyes silently reflecting his distaste for the tailor. The lawman led him away by the elbow, saying, "Let me get you a cider, sir, and we'll leave this fellow in peace to find what lawful pursuits he may like."

He caught the tavern keeper's eye, calling out, "A cider for my friend here, and perhaps some assistance to that gentleman to get him to a bed for the night?" The tailor returned to his seat and grimly accepted the tankard of cider, watching with a scowl as the tavern keeper bent and helped the protesting Cooper to his feet, and up the stairs toward his room.

Calabar stood to follow, and saw the sheriff standing at the front door, keeping an eye on both him and the tailor. Looking at Calabar, he nodded once more, a wisp of compassion visible in his expression, and then turned and left the tavern.

Calabar climbed the stairs wearily behind the tavern keeper and Cooper's bulky, nearly inert form, feeling as though the road ahead of him once again contained unknowable twists and turns, and was populated with a myriad of unavoidable dangers.

Chapter 12

In the month since the sale of Cooper's indigo, Calabar's life had fallen into a quiet routine. He rose with the dawn, having become inured to the discomfort of his too-soft bed, brought the tray of bread and cheese and cider into his room, and broke fast in solitude. He then dressed in the fashion that Cooper had shown him, slipping his new shirt on over his head, drawing on his stockings and trousers, fastening the simple buckles at his knees and slipping his feet into the shoes – which still left his feet aching after a day of walking through the town – tying his cravat, and then buttoning up his waistcoat and placing his hat upon his head.

Though a far more elaborate process than rising and working in what clothes he had slept in, as he'd done in his previous life, he still found that he felt underdressed somehow as the eyes of children on the street followed him, wide and wondering.

The tavern keeper still had scarcely a word for him, other than to grunt and frown when Calabar took his accustomed seat in the corner of the tavern at supper time. Nonetheless, Calabar gave the man a respectful bow of the head as he passed out onto the street.

Cooper was not yet about, but Calabar did not expect to see him until later in the morning anyway. In the weeks since the last ship to London had sailed, they had purchased several more shipments of indigo bricks together, their price guided by Calabar's knowledge and ability to gauge the quality of the product. While there was nothing available to rival the final shipment from Greene's plantation, there was still sufficient quantity of reasonably good indigo to fill many barrels in a warehouse by the docks as they awaited the next outbound ship.

Of course, Cooper was established in other markets beyond just indigo. Rice attracted his attention, but there were many entrenched merchants already buying the production of nearly all of the local plantations, so there was little opportunity for him there. "It's like being the last to a dinner party," he'd remarked to Calabar. "There may be a seat at the table for you, if you're lucky, but by the time the pudding comes around the table, all you find on the platter are a few crumbs and scraps."

He had somewhat better luck with timber, which was in higher demand than usual, due to worries about access to the customary markets up the coast. The harbor at Boston was still sealed off by the royal navy, and Governor Gage's troops patrolled the streets of that beleaguered town.

Cooper told Calabar, somewhat cynically, "I've answered appeals for relief, sending supplies up to the people of Massachusetts Bay Colony, both out of a sense of duty to my friends in those parts, and because so long as they can be supported in spite of the closure of Boston Harbor, there will be no resolution, and our own goods will go all the dearer . . . so I spend less on relief than I gain in higher prices at the docks."

This logic was a good deal more convoluted than Calabar could make sense of, but he was glad to hear that the prices of things sold and shipped from town might go higher yet. Deep in his heart, he still nurtured a bright flame of hope that he might be able to earn enough in this season of trading to be able to offer Master Greene a price sufficient to purchase freedom for Affey and Fantee.

While he still hadn't mustered the boldness to put it into motion, he had a plan in mind. He knew that having the money in hand would make it far easier to execute, and so he kept telling himself that he was only waiting for the next shipment of indigo to go out, and for Cooper to deliver to him his share of the profit, and that he would then be able to speak up.

In more truthful moments with himself, though, he acknowledged that he was terrified that his plan would fall into pieces at one point or another. He intended to find out from Cooper where he might be able to find Jake – of the brothers who'd thought him a runaway, and had later delivered Greene's indigo to the market here in town – and to then beseech Jake to inquire of Master Greene what price he might like for his household domestic and her baby.

Armed with that knowledge, he hoped to arrange for Jake to purchase them, and then free them, to Calabar's care in town. Greene need never know that his old slave Jupiter was involved at all, and the whole family might then remove themselves to some distant parts, where they would be safe from all future encounters with their former master, as well as observing the law of the colony that demanded their departure.

As he walked down the street, Calabar spied a couple of other freedmen in a back alley between shops, their reasonably decent, if worn, clothes and dark skins marking their peculiar status in society more clearly than a brand upon their foreheads would have done. The two men raised their hands in greeting, and Calabar returned the gesture reflexively.

"You be new in this town," remarked the first, pointing at

the still-crisp seams on Calabar's waistcoat. The man pressed his palm to his own chest, fingers spread wide. "I be Little Pete, been free three year." Little Pete put his hand on his smaller companion's shoulder. "This be Simbee, good fellow, don't be talk much."

Offering his hand now in a handshake, the large man asked, "And you be?"

"I am be called Jupiter, but my name be Calabar," he replied, accepting the offered hand. "Been free just a month." He added quizzically, "You been free for three year? I been told that freedmen must leave the colony within one year."

Little Pete theatrically looked left, and then right, putting his finger up to his mouth, which crooked in a smile. "You not be tell Master Sheriff, he not be ask after me." He leaned back against the wall behind him. "I not be around town much anyway, so Master Sheriff not have to be knowing that I been free for so long."

Calabar raised an eyebrow in silent question. Little Pete motioned him back into the alley, out of sight of the street. "There be places beyond the reach of the white masters, places where a freedman be breathing free, working free, eating free, living free."

Calabar retorted, "I be living free, eating, working here in town."

Little Pete shook his head vehemently. "You be passing, and that be all. Only last so long as they have use for you. After that, you be finding that life here not as free as it looking."

Calabar frowned, answering, "I been met the sheriff himself, when a tailor wanted me be gone. Sheriff told tailor I be free to be here, tailor be leaving me in peace."

Little Pete shrugged. "It be your life to risk, but I been seeing this before. Where I be living, no papers, some not even be having them anyway." He winked. "Some been making their own freedom, not been waiting for they masters."

The idea sent a thrill down Calabar's spine. Runaways! He shuddered visibly, answering, "That be no way to live, friend. All time, be worrying be caught, be whipped, be having ears cut off or worse, be sent back to masters with chains and watching eye."

He shook his head violently, as though trying to rid himself of the memories of what he'd seen in such circumstances. "Seen boy come back, no skin left on him back. Boy been strung up by master not long after, left to swing in wind until crows cut him down."

He shuddered again, asking, "There be whole plantation of runaways? Sheriff be making all to burn, nobody live, papers or no papers."

Little Pete listened gravely, answering, "There be no talk to Master Sheriff about them freedmen or others who be living away, no talking to any white man, or he be coming and make all burn, as you been said."

Calabar raised his hands before himself, saying, "I not be talking to any white man to make your plantation burn, but I not be coming to burn with it when they do be find it."

Simbee spoke now, saying in a quiet, almost girlish voice, "If we burn, I coming to find you." His dark eyes glittered in the shadows of the alley, and Calabar felt a fresh chill rush up his spine.

Little Pete put a hand on Simbee's shoulder again, admonishing the smaller man, "There be no cause for be threatening Mister Calabar, Simbee." He looked at Calabar. "Is there be?"

Calabar shook his head quickly, wishing for the encounter to be finished, wishing that he could return to the world of the unwelcoming table at the tavern and the company of the friendly, if naïve, Mister Cooper, wishing that he could have the comfort of discussing with the milliner his fierce rage at the entire institution of slavery.

Little Pete nodded slowly, and Simbee faded back behind the large man again, though his eyes continued to follow Calabar maliciously. After taking a deep breath, Little Pete said, "I be seeing man caught after run away one time. It been bad to see, no thing I been wanting to see again."

He closed his eyes for a long moment, and then continued. "He been work at rice plantation where I been work, but when master's wife been fallen sick, he slipped away, been gone for almost fortnight. They say he been poison master's wife, but she been sick all time, not been poisoned. Still, the master been said he been poison her, so he been tied to a post, then he been whip until they been no more to whip, then he been hang, and after he been hang, they been cut off his head, and they been put it on a pole in front of the slave quarters."

The big man fell silent after this lengthy exposition, his face somber. He added, almost as an afterthought, "I not been want run away. I been quiet, been work hard, been earn papers. But I not be judge them who be want run away. Just be quiet, be work hard, be help when I been able."

Little Pete and Calabar regarded each other, each of them clearly having more to say, but both unwilling to speak any further. Finally, Simbee spoke from the shadows, "No free man or runaway will be hang for the you, Mister Calabar. Know you that." He grabbed Little Pete's elbow and drew the big man back into the darkness of the alleyway, until they both disappeared behind the shop.

Chapter 13

Calabar returned to his room, shaken but more determined than before to find a way to carry himself and his family away from the horrors that seemed to lurk for them throughout the colony. He sat on his bed and dug into the pile of folded clothes on the shelf beside it, pulling out the leather purse from where he had concealed it.

He spilled its contents out onto the bed beside him, carefully counting up the guineas, then the half-crowns, shillings, and pence. As Cooper had warned him they would, the small coins had proliferated, but he counted them no less carefully than he had the heavy guineas.

He struggled to remember the mathematical relationships between the coins – how many half-crowns made up a pound again? – but finally came up to a total that he felt he could trust. Dressing, housing, and feeding himself had consumed a dreadful amount of money, but he was hopeful that Cooper was correct, and that he would replenish what he had and then some as they sold the rest of their indigo stocks in the coming days.

Would it be enough? Would Master Greene have learned to value Affey's skill in the kitchen, her ability to mix and apply poultices, and the gentle care she had always supplied his father? Would he assign any value at all to the baby?

As Calabar considered the possibilities, he heard a scratching at his door and quickly flipped the top edge of his blanket over the scattered coins. The door opened, and the tavern keeper's wench, a wild-looking indentured girl with hair the color of cooked yams, appeared, a pitcher in her hand. She emitted a small shriek of surprise at finding Calabar in his room, and she splashed water out of the pitcher across the floor as she jumped. For his part, Calabar found that his heart was pounding in his throat at her unexpected appearance.

"Och, and himself might ha' warned me tha' ye were within," she exclaimed to Calabar, shaking her head, her lips pursed, as she entered the room and refilled the wash basin under Calabar's single small window. Her eyes darted back toward Calabar as she poured the water, his presence seeming to make her uneasy.

He was keenly aware that he sat concealing wealth that the girl could only ever dream of possessing, and he kept his eyes on her as steadily as he could, not daring to move, lest the coins clink together and betray his hoard. He felt instinctively that she would not hesitate to tear apart his room in his absence and rob him of everything, should she become aware that he had something worth stealing.

He knew well from his time in the alleyway before he'd met Cooper, that even the lowliest white person would face little or no consequence for robbing a former slave. What was his, he would have to preserve by his own efforts. Then, he'd had nothing worth preserving or stealing; now, he most emphatically did.

After she finished filling his washbasin, he said gravely, "Thank you, miss."

She seemed about to make a sketch of a curtsey, before she visibly reminded herself that he was owed no such gesture of respect, even from her like, and instead said curtly, "If ye'll be leavin' yer door open while yer within, it'll save me the shock of me life in the future."

Calabar said nothing, but after she'd left, he rose and closed the door behind her before sweeping up the coins with which he hoped to bring out of bondage those whom he loved. Secreting the purse away again, he glanced out the window and decided that it was likely late enough in the day that Cooper might be awaiting him in the tavern.

Downstairs, the merchant was indeed already seated at his customary table, a steaming cup of tea before him. Spying Calabar, he lifted the cup with a pleased smile. "How now, Mister Jupiter? Will you join me for a cup of tea?" Leaning forward to speak under his voice as Calabar sat, he added, "I've fortified mine in the manner in you once told me that Mister Green liked his. 'Tis a cheerful addition, and I thank you for the suggestion."

Calabar smiled quickly in answer, though he could still feel his hands trembling slightly at the nerve-wracking morning he'd had. "I not be wanting tea today, Mister Cooper," he said quietly.

"'I do not want tea today, Mister Cooper,'" the merchant corrected him quickly. "'Tis important that you learn to speak well, that those around you will not think less of you, and perceive that they may take unfair advantage of your prior condition of servitude."

"I do not want tea today, Mister Cooper," Calabar said in rote repetition. Cooper had been insisting on helping Calabar to improve his English for better than a fortnight now, and although the freedman appreciated the merchant's intention, he had not spent much time or effort on absorbing the lessons. Unless his improved speech could change the color of his skin, Calabar could not see that it would appreciably change how people treated him.

Cooper had also hinted that Calabar ought to undertake learning numbers, and even reading, though he thought that it might still be illegal teach a black man to read. Calabar could appreciate the advantages, but it seemed to him that the prize of reading and writing stood high atop a mountain, one that he was too consumed with other matters to focus on climbing.

Cooper took no notice of Calabar's mood, saying, "Today, we make our fortune complete. The indigo we've stockpiled should sell for nearly a thousand guineas, of which some three hundred fifty will be profit. Why, by the end of the day, you may have tripled your wealth!"

That thought did cheer Calabar up substantially – while he'd been aware that they had purchased a large quantity of indigo, he also knew that it was of no better than fair to middling quality, and had not expected to earn very much as his share. He mentally halved, halved again, and halved a third time the prospective profit that Cooper had mentioned to arrive at his share, and was so surprised at the result that he missed entirely what the merchant said next.

As Cooper looked at him, obviously expecting a reply, Calabar said, "Beg pardon?" That was one phrase he had learned, at least.

Cooper repeated, "I should like for you to accompany me again to the docks as we sell off the indigo today. I am told that there will actually be two bidders for the lots, and I think it would be advantageous to have you there to attest to the quality of each."

Calabar nodded. "I be glad to come."

Cooper corrected him again, "'I'd be glad to come,'" and then continued, "Excellent. We have four lots in all, consisting of over a thousand bricks of indigo, so if you can briefly demonstrate the quality of each lot, it will move the whole process along more smartly."

Calabar nodded again, repeating carefully, "I'd be glad to come."

Cooper clapped his hands happily, exclaiming, "Capital!" He added, more quietly, "This sale will come at a very handy time, as I am running low on precisely that."

He sighed, continuing, "I have nearly all of my capital tied up in the indigo, as I have wanted to make the most of our partnership. We have no assurance that British ports will be open to our goods by the time the next season begins, nor even that our own ports will remain in operation. I read dire things out of the Boston news-papers, friend, and I will be glad to have my hands on money that rings true, should the dark days they foretell come to pass."

"Are you thinking that it be come to war between the colony and Britain?"

Cooper was so intent on his reply that he forgot to correct Calabar's grammar. He answered carefully and in nearly a whisper, "I think it is already all but an open war; we await only the first shot. Of course, there is no chance that the colonies can prevail over the home government; the Crown's naval power is unparalleled on all the seas, and the militias that have started playing at drill in Massachusetts Bay Colony are no match for the might of the King's armies."

He grimaced. "However, such unrest is no good for the trade, at least not the honest trade. A filthy smuggler can make his fortune at such a time, but I have neither the inclination nor the experience to walk on that side of the docks."

Sitting back and resuming a more normal tone, Cooper said, "So, today we will put our attentions toward selling our indigo; tomorrow will worry about itself."

Calabar nodded agreeably, though his mind roiled with questions about how the conflict that Cooper predicted might impact his plans to build a quiet life with his family. It seemed hardly fair to him that some troublemakers in far-off Boston could have so much influence on the way of the world that a humble freedman here should have to worry for the future.

Chapter 14

If the evening before had been a scene of unprecedented merriment and celebration for Cooper and Calabar, the morning after the sale of the final lot of their investment in indigo dawned quietly, with an overcast sky hiding the sunrise.

Calabar had only had cider, but plenty of it, while Cooper had downed cup after cup of the finest rum that the tavern held. The freedman rose as usual when what light that was visible through the clouds illuminated his room. He washed his face and dressed in his normal mode, and took the extra precaution of moving the now-bulging purse to a different location in his room, under a folded spare blanket on bench at the foot of his bed.

The sales yesterday had gone even better than Cooper had hoped, the bidding back and forth between buyers helping to increase the final price they got for each of the lots of the indigo. Despite their lower quality than the lot from Greene's plantation, yesterday's lots had sold for nearly as much. Cooper had practically chortled with glee as he counted out Calabar's share – a small sack full of guineas, and a few half-crowns to round it all out.

Calabar knew that he had the price of his family's freedom in the room with him, and the thought filled him with a dreadful thrill of excitement and fear. He might even have sufficient money left over to provide a decent living for them until they could find some new means of earning income.

He fetched his meal from outside the door and sat quietly on his bed to eat it, his mind racing in the clarity of morning. It was time to put his dearest-held dream into motion – looking for the release from bondage of his dear Affey and daughter Fantee. He did not venture out onto the street this day, afraid that his thoughts would be visible on his face, and fearful that by revealing them he might endanger their likelihood of becoming reality.

Instead, he set his tray back outside his room, closed the door, and lay on top of his bed, not even noticing how normal its soft comfort had become to him. He went over plans and alternatives, rehearsing possibilities for setbacks and how he might overcome them. The biggest sticking point was where, exactly, his family might find to live, and in the end, he decided that he had little choice but to ask Mister Cooper's advice.

Noting that the clouds had thinned and the sun was high in the sky, he decided to go down to the tavern to see whether Cooper had come to sup yet. He found his partner at the table, looking ragged and weary, a news-paper before him.

"Good morning, Mister Cooper," Calabar said quietly, noting the change in Cooper's demeanor from the previous night's revelry. "Is the news be so bad?"

Cooper looked blearily up from his news-paper, saying in a quiet voice, "Just, 'Is the news so bad,' Mister Jupiter. And yes, the news is grim."

He held up the news-paper and read aloud, "By letters from Connecticut, and by several credible gentlemen arrived from thence, we are informed, that there were not less than forty thousand men in motion, and under arms, on their way to Boston, on Saturday, Sunday, and Monday last, having heard a false report that the troops had fired upon Boston, and killed several of the inhabitants."

He lowered the news-paper for a moment, interjecting, "'Tis a wholly believable rumor to have spread, and likely just a matter of time before it comes to pass."

Raising the paper back up, he continued reading, "Twelve hundred arrived at Hartford from Farmington and other places forty miles beyond Hartford, on Sunday last, on their way to this place, so rapidly did the news fly. But being informed by express that it was a false report, they returned home, declaring themselves ready at a minute's warning to arm again, and fight for their country, and distressed brethren of Boston."

He scanned further down into the same article, muttering to himself, " . . . Governor Hutchinson, so certain that the tea will be paid, and all will be well again, ha! . . . young fools, just dumb luck that the one killed the other, and did not touch off the war in that moment . . . cannon spiked by the royal navy and restored by the rebels, huh . . . " Finally, he found the passage he wanted to continue with.

"The Newport Mercury of last Monday says that 'the alarm which went through the country last Saturday and yesterday overnight, reached New-York on Monday and had not the accounts been soon contradicted, is it very certain that there would have been sixty or eighty thousand men in arms near Boston, in two days, not as some Tories infamously insinuate, for the purpose of rebellion, but in defense of all that is valuable, dear, holy, and sacred."

Folding the news-paper and setting it back down onto the table, Cooper shook his head somberly. "So, now we sit with open warfare at a hair-trigger, ready to take up arms with deadly purpose 'at a minute's warning,' and so many men that no matter how ill-trained, poorly led, or little disciplined, they should run over the King's forces like so many ants over a lion."

He sighed deeply. "And though we have had no such alarms yet in these parts, the same passions inflame all too many hearts here as well. Those like you and I, who should prefer to simply trade in peace and open friendship with all parties, shall soon be forced to choose a side, if only to avoid being accused of treason by the other."

He raised a finger to get the tavern keeper's attention. "May I get another cup of your small ale, and a cider for my friend?"

The tavern keeper smirked knowingly. "You'll be taking it easy today, I see."

Cooper nodded with a resigned expression on his face. "Yesterday was a day for celebration; it is only right that it be followed by a day for reflection."

"Just as you say, sir," the tavern keeper replied, and went to fetch their drinks, still smirking to himself.

As he moved away, Cooper muttered under his breath again, " . . . smug little . . . " He trailed off as the tavern keeper turned, asking, "Was there something else you were wanting, sir? Perhaps a bite to eat?"

Cooper raised his hands in negation. "Just the ale, thank you."

The tavern keeper returned to the counter to fetch their drinks, and the merchant continued his earlier comments to Calabar. "It won't be enough, either, to simply avoid being accused of treason. Sellers will want to know that you share their sentiments, and buyers likewise. Whichever side one picks, when it is all over, I don't doubt that there will be reprisals and hard feelings, and it may be a score of years before business will be conducted without the question arising: 'Rebel or King's man?'"

He sighed as the tavern keeper brought over the ale and cider. "These are hard times, my friend," he said, and the tavern keeper, overhearing him, nodded sagely.

"Indeed they are, hard and strange." He looked significantly at Calabar as he set the freedman's cider before him. Cooper glanced up at the man with a frown.

"Thank you for the ale, kind sir." The flat tone of his voice left no doubt that this was a dismissal and not an invitation to further discussion, and the man turned on his heel without further comment or expression.

After the tavern keeper retreated to his counter to stand, scowling and wiping mugs clean with his dishrag, Cooper said quietly, "I cannot make sense of that man's behavior. He is making good money by your presence under his roof, with a paid bed that he need not send his boy out to find occupants for every night, and a table where we regularly dine in good fashion. Your money in his cash-box spends the same as mine, and I see no lack of other customers in the tavern for your presence."

Calabar said slowly, "I might be reminding him of some other person who look like me." He held his arm up, gesturing at the dark color of his skin. "Not all mans be so good as you be at seeing past the skin, into the mind and heart."

Cooper appeared moved by the freedman's words, and did not so much as hint at giving a correction to his partner's grammar. He hid his emotion in the bottom of his cup, drinking deeply and slowly, and then setting the empty cup down gently.

"Thank you, my friend," he said. "'Tis true that I have come to care less of the color of your skin, but that most fellows I know would be hard pressed to look at you and see anything else."

He sighed. "'Tis an awful waste of your capacity, of course, to remain ignorant of the ways in which you might serve others, beyond the mere brute strength of your back. Mind you, the measure of a man is not found solely in his service to others, but 'tis a necessary condition to earning your way in this world. Too many take the measure of a man on the basis of irrelevant aspects such as how dusky the skin, or how humble the birth."

He waved his hands dismissively. "We need not discuss the depths of philosophy today, though. We've more pressing matters that must be resolved." He eyed Calabar, a familiar look of shrewd assessment coming over his face. "Is it still in your mind to attempt to purchase the liberty of your wife and child from your old master?"

Calabar's head spun at the sudden and unexpected direction of Cooper's conversation. After a brief hesitation, he nodded tightly. "I be thinking that I should have enough guineas in my purse now for what they're worth."

Cooper nodded approvingly. "I don't doubt it, after yesterday's profits. From what you've told me of your life at the plantation, I gather that she is employed as a kitchen domestic, and that your daughter is not yet of an age to serve?"

"Yes, sir," Calabar answered, still uneasy at the realization that the other man had been paying sufficient attention to have developed a clear idea of Calabar's situation prior to his manumission. He wasn't accustomed to any white man giving the account of his time in bound service more acknowledgement than, perhaps, an uneasy nod.

A look of distaste came over Cooper's face. "I have seen enough auctions at the docks to have a fair sense of what a skilled house slave is worth there. As for the baby, she is of no use to anyone without her mother, so it may be possible to convince Mister Greene to just add her to the deal at no additional cost."

He looked sharply at Calabar. "She's yours of course, and there is no chance that she's old Mister Greene's?" As the freedman's eyebrows lowered in anger, the merchant held up his hands in a mollifying gesture.

"I apologize; I meant no slight, but needed to ask to learn whether he might place some value on her above just another mouth to feed, and one that is yet years away from any possible use."

Calabar still felt a small, hot ember of rage in his heart at Cooper for even asking the question, but he did his best to suppress it. He shook his head emphatically. "My Anna never been laying with Mister Greene, and she would have told me if he ever been laying a hand on her." He shook his head again. "The baby is mine."

Cooper nodded. "Good, good, that makes things more straightforward." Calabar realized that his hands had clenched of their own accord into fists, and knowing that the merchant meant only to help, he made a conscious effort to open them as Cooper continued, "Should you like me to approach your former master and learn whether he might be willing to part with your Anna and the babe?"

Calabar's eyes narrowed for a moment in thought. "I been thinking to ask you or the cart-driver, Jake, to talk to Master Greene, but I been thinking that he might be anger at our partnership."

Cooper nodded thoughtfully. "He might indeed resent the

fact that he failed to see any value in you, but I helped you to earn your whole auction price in a matter of a few weeks and then some. However, unless you have been spreading word of the details of our arrangement –" Calabar shook his head in emphatic negation "– I could just as easily tell him that I want to buy Anna for my own purposes, and that my interest was driven purely by your testimony to her qualities."

Pressing his palms together and lifting them contemplatively to his mouth, he added, "If he were to go along with it, I would, of course, sign their manumissions just as swiftly as ever I could, and deliver them up to you as freedmen."

A lump formed in Calabar's throat at the prospect of achieving in a single stroke all that he had dared to dream. Struggling to speak, he said, "Thank you, Mister Cooper. That be more than I been thinking I could ask from you."

Cooper nodded gravely. "You have made this an exceptionally prosperous season for me, and I feel that I owe you more than just the profits we have split." He regarded the freedman quietly for a moment, and then said, "Perhaps our friend the milliner had the right of it when he said that you've already paid enough in the stolen years of your life; he gave you your first hat, and with another smile from fortune, I can help to give you back your family."

He raised a single finger. "If we are to pursue this course, though, you will need to stay here, and I shall need to carry your purse as though it were my own, so that I can offer him money that clinks, and not just my word as a gentleman."

He smiled at Calabar, a knowing twinkle in his eye. "A man who is trying to lay his hands on capital for the conversion of a plantation from one crop to another is more likely to see sweet reason when he looks for it in the face of our sovereign on a coin of gold."

Calabar saw at once that this plan would require him to entrust Cooper with his fortune, but he had little reservation about doing so. He had earned it for so little effort that it hardly seemed real to him that he had it in any case, and he had furthermore received it from this same man's unhesitating hands.

Still, he knew that, just as was the case with the serving wench, should Cooper simply disappear with his money, he would have little or no recourse in the sheriff or any other institution of the white world. As a slave, he had had virtually no rights; as a freedman, his situation was only slightly improved, where the law was concerned.

He nodded once, decisively and sharply. "Let us do this. I go and fetch my purse."

Chapter 15

After he watched Cooper disappear out of town down the track toward Greene's newly inherited plantation, carrying Calabar's heavy purse, the freedman had nothing to do but wait. His heart insisted on rising into his throat, pounding with a mixture of terror and excitement. As much out of a desire to distract himself as anything else, he wanted to find someone to speak with to help to pass the time until – he hoped – Cooper should return with Affey and Fantee.

Almost as if of their own will, he found that his feet carried him to the old milliner's shop, which he'd not visited since the man had gifted him with his hat. The shutters were closed, but he knocked at the door of the shop, which creaked open freely at his touch.

His brow lowering in concern, he leaned toward the door, calling out, "Be you there?" There was no answer, and he pushed the door open the rest of the way, stepping into the shadowed, dark shop. He called out again into the darkness, "Mister Allbright? It be your friend Jupiter. Be you here?"

A stirring noise at the back of the shop caught his attention and he stepped forward, straining to see in the limited light that filtered in through the closed shutters. As he did so, he stumbled against a hat rack, knocking it over with a clatter and sending hats spilling and bouncing across the floor.

The old milliner suddenly sat upright from a pallet at the back corner of the shop, shouting, "Who is it? What do you want of me? I warn you, I am not afraid to defend what's mine!" Calabar could see a flash of steel in the other man's hands, reflections from what looked like a very large knife.

Backing up and raising his hands to show that they were empty, Calabar answered, "It be me, sir, your friend Jupiter."

The other man grunted and raised himself to stand and peer out with one eye glinting in the little light that reached it, the other eye a dark, empty socket. Even from the front of the shop, Calabar could smell the sweet-sour smell of last night's rum in the air, emanating like a cloud from the milliner's very skin. Mister Greene had occasionally smelled the same way, particularly right after harvest, a memory that struck Calabar vividly as he waited for the old milliner to respond.

"Jupiter . . . Jupiter . . . I don't remember a friend Jupiter." The old man shuffled forward, picking up a rag from the counter as he did so and tying it around his head, covering his bad eye. Peering at Calabar, he waved two fingers in the air, as though drawing the memories out of the recesses of his mind.

"Ah, yes," he finally said. "The freedman, late of the indigo manufacture, now employed with Mister Cooper as a merchant of the same. Gave you that hat, didn't I?"

"Indeed," said Calabar. "I be come to share news and pass time, though if this not be a good moment . . . "

"Certainly, 'tis a fine moment, if you can but wait for the few minutes it will take an old man to be prepared to receive company."

"I be glad for a wait, yes. I will be outside."

"Aye, and thank you kindly." Calabar exited the shop and closed the door behind him, leaning against the frame as he waited. He had begun to have second thoughts about coming to visit Allbright – the old man seemed to be plagued with problems of his own, if the persistent air of old drink that seemed to accompany him was any indication.

On the other hand, outside of Cooper, he was the closest thing to a friend that Calabar had among the people of the town. Little Pete and the few other freedmen Calabar had encountered had been less than warm toward him, apparently sharing resentment at Calabar's easy fortune. And, of course, before Calabar had found his fortune, none of the freedmen had been eager to provide him with any assistance.

The old man's outright anger at the whole institution of slavery also gave Calabar much to think about – he'd always just known that this was the way of the world. Some men labored at the command of others, and sometimes the commands were legitimized through the ownership of the laborers by those issuing the commands.

Other times, as with the serving wench at the tavern, it was a matter of indenture, but so long as the commands were being given and obeyed, he didn't see what the practical difference was. Of course, the situation of a slave was worsened by the laws that applied to slaves – and freedmen – nearly all of which denied them the most basic of protections that were afforded to even someone like the girl who fetched his breakfast and refilled his wash water.

He was startled out of these thoughts as the shutters over one window and then the other banged open from the inside, and he cautiously re-entered the shop when the old milliner swung the door open and called out cheerfully, "There we go – open for business, open for a good gossip."

Gone was the bleary-eyed wreck of a man who had jumped up and menaced him in the darkness. Instead, the milliner had changed into clean clothing and had a fresh cloth folded and tied neatly over his bad eye. Though he still wore the rough stubble of a few days' passage since a visit to the barber, his uncovered eye sparkled with good humor.

The hat racks stood in tidy order, with no hint of the disturbance that had rousted the old man from his bed, and the light streaming through the open windows made the shop feel like a different place. A small fire already crackled in the hearth at the back of the shop, and Calabar could see a kettle suspended over it, just starting to steam.

"I'd offer you a cider," Allbright said, "but I seem to have finished the last of mine in the night. Still, gossip and questions can take place as easily over a pipe as over a cup."

Seeing the look of confusion on Calabar's face, the old man laughed. "What, have you never tried the tobacco? 'Tis a capital crop in these parts, and is moreover responsible for plenty of capital." The milliner cackled with laughter at his own witticism, until he began to cough, his eye streaming as he slapped his knee.

When he'd recovered himself, he continued to stifle an occasional guffaw as he produced a pipe from under the counter, along with a small sack of aromatic tobacco. He remarked, "Most folk take their tobacco as snuff, but I've become partial to simply smoking it in the fashion of the Indians, through a pipe. Stimulates the humors, ensures that I get enough to eat."

Calabar watched with fascination as the old man packed the

bowl of the pipe with shredded tobacco leaf, pressing it delicately into the pipe with his thumb so that it was compressed into the bottom of the bowl while still leaving enough loose space that it would draw – not unlike the small stove that Affey would cook over at the slave quarters.

Allbright reached down to the hearth and drew out a stick that was aglow in embers at one end. Touching it to the tobacco in the pipe that he held clutched in his teeth, he drew in a deep breath, and the embers glowed more brightly, lighting the tobacco with a small, bright flame. He exhaled a moment later, a cloud of aromatic smoke encircling his head. Sniffing the sharp reek of the smoke, Calabar realized that part of the scent that surrounded the old milliner was probably the stale smell of old pipes, and that it was not all just due to an immoderate consumption of rum.

The milliner withdrew the pipe from his mouth and offered it, stem first, to Calabar. "You want to try it?" The freedman looked at the pipe, uncertainty written across his face. "Go ahead," the milliner urged. "You might not like it, but at least then you'll know whether you need a new vice."

Calabar accepted the pipe from the old man's hands. Placing the stem in his mouth, he accidentally released a small breath of air up into the pipe, resulting in a small shower of sparks flying up out of the bowl, and a puff of smoke. It was acrid at this close range, and Calabar's eyes began to water immediately.

Allbright smiled and mimed inhaling a big breath. Calabar did his best to imitate the other man's technique, and was rewarded with a chest full of burning, vile-tasting smoke that poured out of his mouth and nose as he gasped and began coughing, desperately handing the pipe back to the milliner. By the time he was done coughing and wheezing, the milliner was again laughing so hard that he began to cough, and the two of them stood hacking for the span of several minutes before either of them could speak again.

When he'd regained his composure, Calabar shook his head, wiping tears away from his eyes. "I not be thinking that I like the tobacco," he said gravely, noticing that his mouth felt like it was coated in ashes.

The milliner had set the stem of the pipe back into his mouth, and replied around it, "No, I don't suppose that most men do when first they try it – but don't give up on it entirely. You may well find that it grows on you over time, and 'tis healthful beyond expectations." He took another deep draw at the pipe and puffed out with his mouth held in a round. Calabar was entranced to see the smoke form a spinning ring in the air for a moment before it dissipated and Allbright smiled at him, a twinkle in his eye.

"Well, enough beating about the bush," the old man said around the stem of the pipe. "You didn't come here to try tobacco or ponder hats, I wager."

"No, sir, I be here on other business." Calabar sketched out the plan in motion for the liberation of his family in brief, hesitant words, almost unwilling to give voice to the hopes he held for the outcome. He concluded, "Even if Mister Cooper be able to purchase them from young Master Greene, I be not knowing what we all be doing. I be having just a few months left before the sheriff will be come for me."

The milliner frowned doubtfully. "Just a few months? For what reason might the sheriff bother with an honest fellow like yourself?"

Calabar recounted the discussion with the sheriff at the

tavern. "So I cannot dream of make my home here for more than next summer, even if Mister Cooper and I be buying, selling more of the indigo."

The older man drew fiercely at his pipe, making the embers in the bowl flare into brightness. He thoughtfully let the smoke trickle out through the corner of his mouth, his eyebrows entangling with each other, so deep was his scowl.

Finally he said, "I am not acquainted with this law that the sheriff cited, but I don't misdoubt that the old tyrant Governor Tryon, or the fool who sits in the government house now, Governor Martin, would have enacted such a violence against the rights of free men." He shook his head, the frown on his face deepening, if anything.

"Be that as it may," he said after a moment's thought, "I wish you all possible joy of your fortune, and hope that your knowledge of your craft may prove to be the undoing of the bondage suffered by your family. Even if Mister Cooper is successful in his quest to secure their purchase and manumission, though, your problems for the remainder of your time here are formidable indeed."

He held up his fingers, ticking off the items as he spoke. "One, you must find a more suitable place to stay than the tavern. Though it suits your needs well enough, it is too bawdy a place for a member of the fairer sex and a babe in arms."

That thought hadn't occurred to Calabar before now, and he was so consumed with thoughts of how to respond to this challenge that he almost missed the old milliner's next point. "Two, you must find suitable employment for yourself, and likely for your wife as well. Finally, you must decide upon a course of action for your long term felicity and health."

Calabar nodded, feeling overwhelmed by it all. It almost seemed as though his life would be simpler if Cooper failed – though he viciously quashed the thought as soon as it crept into his mind – and that as hard as the past month had been, it was just preparation for the months ahead.

Allbright smiled widely, though. "I believe that, should your business associate return in triumph, with your wife and babe, all the rest will fall into place readily enough." He peered past Calabar, as though he were checking to ensure that nobody was lurking outside of the windows of the shop to hear his words, and then leaned forward, speaking in a quieter tone.

"I have reason to believe that the governor and perhaps the sheriff, too, will soon be too consumed with their own troubles to bother with you." Calabar's confusion must have been evident on his face, as the old man raised his hand and nodded quickly. "I suspect that you know little of the brewing conflict with the Crown across these colonies?"

Calabar shook his head slightly. "I been hearing Mister Cooper and others talk about trouble in Boston, yell about tea like that, but I know no more about these thing."

Allbright sat back and pulled at his pipe thoughtfully. After releasing another slow trickle of smoke out of the side of his mouth, he said quietly, "It will soon come to warfare, and it is only a matter of chance whether the spark is struck in Boston, or in New-York . . . or here. The tinder of rebellion is dry and stacked high throughout the colonies, and once the flame is lit, it is unlikely to be quenched."

He took another pull at his pipe and continued, smoke giving his words momentary form in the air. "The Crown has abused its authority in these colonies, imposing its will without bothering to ask our opinion in many diverse matters. Most damning, the Parliament sees fit to demand taxes of us, but the King refuses to permit the colonies to have a voice in setting those taxes."

He frowned deeply, the wrinkles in his face deepening into leathery, shadowed creases. "They use our shores as a convenient dumping ground for anything that they cannot impose elsewhere, whether goods – such as the tea that was sunk in Boston Harbor and elsewhere – or men, such as our little-loved governor."

Calabar asked, puzzled, "Can you not send them back?"

The old man shook his head, his frown turning into a sardonic smile. "Nay, we tried that at Boston, and the King sent an army over to compel the subjugation of the people there. And an army will, eventually, find opposition by another army, 'tis just the nature of things."

His eyes took on a haunted look. "Two armies facing each other in opposition will always wind up shooting at one another, until only one remains in the field, and the other has laid down its arms to rest under the bloodstained earth."

Shaking off his gloom, he sat up and arched an eyebrow at Calabar. "So, you can see why I think that the governor is unlikely to take much of an interest in a single freedman and his family."

Calabar frowned. "What of sheriff, and what of his friend, be tailor?"

"Might make trouble for you, but they, too, are likely to be consumed by the impact of the rebellion, should it catch fire here." The old man grimaced and leaned forward again. "You must give me your word as a man of honor that what I say here does not pass from your lips beyond this room."

Calabar frowned in confusion again. "Please, sir, I do not understand."

"I mean to share confidences with you, and must know that you will not reveal them to my ruin and that of others as well."

Calabar nodded slowly, still not sure what exactly he was agreeing to.

Allbright seemed satisfied, though, as he leaned even closer in toward Calabar. "Some of the organizers in this district of the Committee of Safety have laid in place a plan to move against the governor within the fortnight. They do not intend him violence, but when undertaking an action of this sort, it is entirely possible that some outcome that was not looked for may result."

"Move against? What way do you move a governor?"

"By overwhelming his guard and reducing the man to no more than just another ordinary citizen, compelled to resign his post and renounce his former duties."

"Be you mean a revolt?" In his shock at the concept, Calabar knew that his grammar would have drawn a sharp rebuke from Cooper, but Allbright merely pressed a finger to his own lips.

"Shhhh. If you will speak treason, mind that you speak it softly, lest the walls tell the Crown of it."

Calabar was careful to use a quieter tone. "I be speak treason by ask you question?"

The milliner looked grave. "Treason is in the ear of he who hears it, and your questions are not ones that may be safely asked aloud, even at the best of times. This is far from those times, and so giving them voice is an act of either recklessness or bravery – or perhaps both."

He frowned, again looking past Calabar through the

windows. "But to answer your question, in a word, yes. Perhaps not quite yet a revolt against the whole of the Crown, mind you, but one against the person of the governor, who has shown that he is unfit to govern by his actions."

He took another pull at his pipe, warming to his subject. "Now, there is little doubt that the old governor, Mister Tryon, bequeathed to his successor a host of difficult troubles, but Governor Martin has shown little capacity for solving them, while demonstrating a positive genius for making difficult matters even worse."

He grinned. "Some of us, though, know a few things about dealing with difficult and corrupt public officers." The pipe flared up again as he inhaled, and he asked, "You have likely heard of the War of the Regulation?" Calabar shook his head, and Allbright continued, "Your old master was on the wrong side of it, so I am not surprised that he said aught of it to you. Of course, he likely didn't think you capable enough to bother telling you what he was doing, either."

The old milliner shrugged. "Well, the long and the short of it was that the Crown's public officers were taking advantage of their positions to line their own pockets. I know of at least one sheriff who simply 'lost' the records of paid taxes, so as to collect them twice. Without a doubt, the original collection went to his personal account-books, and not into the county's coffers."

Calabar felt shock at the realization that slaves and freedmen were not the only people to be treated with manifest injustice of this nature – those in positions of power seemed to abuse that power universally. He realized that it was perhaps not only the color of their victims' skin that drove the abuse, but the simple fact that they held power over others.

Certainly, a master held more power over his slaves than the sheriff held over the people of his county, but it wasn't difficult to see a broader pattern. His thoughts were interrupted by the old man peering at him inquisitively. "Is my story already so dull that you should like to be elsewhere? It appears that your mind has already wandered away; should you follow it?"

Calabar shook his head vehemently. "No, I be learning and thinking, and be want to learn more. I will attend you more close now."

Allbright nodded, a smile twitching at the edges of his mouth. "See that you do – 'tis a worthy tale, I think."

Sitting back and putting the pipe back into his mouth, the old man continued. "Some of us had had enough of the Crown's officials using the power of their offices for their own benefit, and so we went down to the colonial court building and made an example of some of the worst of them."

Calabar looked up sharply and Allbright said quickly, "Oh, we didn't kill any of them, but we turned their desks into a shambles, and dragged the men responsible out into the streets. The judge had before him a number of cases pertaining to some of our Regulators, and they were sitting untried on his docket, so we asked him to move them up."

He snorted. "The sneak made an excuse about needing to get something from his chambers, and then made off with himself into the night. Some of us got a bit exercised in our frustration at his escape, and so when we laid hands on a couple of lawyers who remained, they were treated pretty roughly. One man was beaten so badly that they had to put his eye back in after, though he was one of the most corrupt of the bunch, so you might say that it were justice done rough."

The old man gestured at the rag tied over his own missing eye. "In a way, that was the incident that led to me losing an eye, although that happened somewhat later, and is a story for another time." He smiled ruefully.

"In any event, after we'd vented our spleens on the lawyers, we made thorough work of the courthouse. One wit even dragged a moldering corpse out of its grave and set it in the lawyers' bar, to give his opinion of how much good they were doing us, alive or dead."

He grimaced. "After that, things got pretty well out of hand. Some of the rowdier boys broke into the same lawyer's house as what lost his eye and drank up all his rum and finer things, which really got them going. We stopped them looting the church, but they cracked the bell there, as justice had gone silent, and so must the English church tower, until justice once again sang sweetly."

He turned his pipe about in his hand, and Calabar noticed that it had gone out, forgotten as the milliner got caught up in telling his story. "So, that was about the whole of that incident, though of course other folks acted in the uprising against corruption in other places. It wasn't until just a few years ago when things really came to a final accounting, though."

He lifted the pipe to his mouth and seemed surprised to find that it did not draw. He grunted and fetched a fresh splinter, relighting the tobacco from the hearth. "Governor Tryon – now off to afflict New-York Colony instead of us – had spent some ten thousand pounds sterling building a great palace for himself at his new capital. He proposed to pay for this extravagance by taxing the ordinary people of the colony, taking bread from their tables to buy crystal and marble for himself."

He spat bitterly into the fire, and it hissed and sizzled for a moment like a thing alive among the embers. "This time, we raised an army, but so did the governor, and what he lacked in numbers, his men made up for in discipline and ferocity. We were out to stampede his forces into retreat, but Governor Tryon himself fired the first shot, mark me, and turned it into a battle. Then he tried to tell a tale of heroism and valor, bragging to all who would listen of how he had saved the colony from the scourge of lawlessness."

He shook his head angrily. "After the first volley of shooting died down, some of our men went to parley. They told us that they would give us two hours to disperse before they would contest the field – but then they commenced to rain down artillery on us, harrying our men into captivity."

He frowned, his mouth pressed tightly. "That was when this happened" – he pointed at the empty eye socket behind its cloth – "and it wasn't long after that we abandoned the field entirely. Some of the leaders were rounded up and hanged for their acts, in defiance of laws that prescribed far lesser punishments."

Allbright's one good eye flashed angrily in the light. "The governor, may his black soul find a suitable place in the hereafter, came away covered in glory, but that lasted only until people examined his actions more closely."

He waved his pipe irritably and noticed that it had again gone out. With a scowl, he turned it over and gave it a good rap on the bottom, knocking the remaining tobacco into the hearth. Turning back to Calabar, he said, "In any event, that is how I lost my eye, and my innocent trust in the government set over us by the

Crown. They may be relied upon only to line their own pockets and look after their particular friends, and the rest of us must be content with their leavings."

Calabar was still absorbing the revelations that the injustices he had experienced as a freed slave were visited in different degree on nearly everyone in the colonies, if the old man's telling of it could be believed. The details differed, but all men, it seemed, suffered the gnawing anxiety that anything they held dear could be violated at a whim.

The realization rocked him to the core, and left him wondering what could be done to right the wrongs of such a wicked world. All that was within his power, he decided, was to pass along the kindness from which he had benefited, wherever he might be able. He was keenly aware that if it weren't for Cooper finding a need for him and seeing advantage to himself in helping Calabar to improve his condition, his own situation would be dire indeed.

And now Cooper was again working to be the builder of a better future, for Calabar's entire family. Such acts could never be repaid, but only emulated. Calabar resolved to look for his own opportunity to improve the lot of someone who had been ill-treated by the world of men. He might not be able to make the whole world a perfect place, but he could improve what was within his own reach.

He looked up to find Allbright examining his face closely, his good eye dancing over the freedman's features. He realized that the old man had been speaking to him, but he hadn't been listening at all – and Allbright knew it, too, a smile cracking his face.

"I'd give a penny to know your thoughts," the old man said, his eye twinkling.

Calabar smiled in response, saying only, "I be grateful for the mercy Mister Cooper and you been showing to me, and I be eager to spread that mercy to others."

Allbright nodded, suddenly thoughtful. "We live in times where mercy is a rare and precious gift, and one worth sharing as widely as is possible."

He slapped his hands on his knees and stood, startling Calabar. "I have kept you all morning, my friend. Mister Cooper should be back from the Greene plantation soon, and I expect that you will want to be at the tavern to receive him, and learn what news he has for you."

Calabar stood, too, realizing that their discussion had taken them deep into the day. He was no closer to solving the problems that Allbright had so succinctly enumerated for him, but he felt, at least, that he had a direction in which to bend his efforts, no matter what news Cooper brought back.

Chapter 16

The tavern was quiet after the mid-day rush of craftsmen, merchants, and workmen coming for a quick cup of cider and a bite to eat before returning to the business of their day. Calabar eased himself into his accustomed seat and the tavern keeper brought him cider and bread without so much as meeting Calabar's eye, setting them on the table as though for someone yet to arrive.

The freedman sighed and picked up the bread, tearing off a chunk to chew on while he thought. While he could not guess whether Cooper would return with his family or empty hands, he would not permit himself to contemplate a future without them. He ached at the memory of cradling Fantee in his arms as she slept, freeing Affey to mend or cook or sleep, unencumbered by the weight of the baby slung about her. He could almost smell the warm, milky scent of her scalp, and feel her soft, pliable ear pressed against his chest.

When she woke, she would grab his finger, her tiny fist clenched tightly around it, and he could remember wondering what labor those small hands would grow to perform. Now, he dared to hope, it would be work of her own choosing, for the benefit of those she loved and cared for.

Calabar's eye fell upon his own hand, holding a crust of bread, and he was surprised to realize how soft the skin of his fingers had become in his time away from the fields. For that matter, the bread that now seemed commonplace, even a little plain, would have represented a gift of royal dimension in his prior life.

He laughed a bit at himself as he noticed, too, that the cuff of his shirt had gotten smudged with something, and felt a moment of irritation at the stain. He had a shirt, with a cuff, and now simply expected that it would remain clean, that his hands would find ease, and that his belly would not grumble for long without his hunger being satisfied.

The future was uncertain, but at least its shape was under his influence. It had been entirely at the mercy of another man's whims before, and now that he had decided upon a course of action in his life, he felt that he finally understood the importance of the concept that had once seemed strange and difficult – freedom.

He could not wait to share it with Affey and the baby.

He took note of the tavern keeper's serving wench, who was huddled furtively in a corner with a rough-looking young man. They were giggling, their heads close together to share confidences, and Calabar saw the lad steal a quick kiss. The wench looked around quickly to see whether anyone had noticed, and caught Calabar's eye. She smiled as though at some private joke and looked away.

Calabar knew in his gut that her smile was drawn from the girl's sense of superiority over him. He felt a flash of irritation at her, paired with a pang of envy for the casual intimacy the boy shared with her. He and Affey had always needed to be circumspect about their relationship, as even so tolerant a master as Mister Greene might take offense at his slaves wasting their time on giggles and kisses.

At the same time, the sight reminded him of the sweetness

of time spent with Affey, the small touches that they shared throughout the day when their paths crossed. Not all love needed to be expressed with kisses and sighs; just a quick sweep of fingers across his shoulder, or a gentle hand on his rough and unshaven cheek, was a hundred times as much an expression of love as anything that might transpire in the corner of a tavern.

The door swung open, rusty hinges protesting, and Cooper stood at the threshold, outlined in a halo of daylight, bringing Calabar's heart leaping into his throat. He stepped inside, and Calabar could see that his face was split into an enormous grin.

A smaller form tentatively followed him into the tavern, and Calabar cried out, "Affey?" Then Affey was in his arms, the baby peering up at him from her sling, pressed between her sobbing parents. She gave a small squeak of protest, and Calabar pulled away slightly to give Fantee more room to breathe.

Affey said, her voice strained and low, "Calabar, this man is my new master, but he said that you bought us from Master Greene, with him only bringing your money to Master Greene." Calabar started to answer, but she looked at him, bewildered, and began weeping again, saying, "He was saying, too, that we are to be free, like you, but Master Greene did not send us away like he did you, so I don't understand how that could be true."

She stood back, holding Calabar at arm's length, and looked him up and down. "And where did you get these clothes? You look like a plantation owner."

She was getting ready to say more, but Calabar raised a single finger and placed it across her lips. "Can I answer your questions before you ask me more?" Over her shoulder, he saw Cooper's smile deepen, and Affey fell back into his arms, nodding silently.

"Thank you, Mister Cooper," he said to the merchant.

Cooper nodded and approached, handing back Calabar's purse, which he was surprised to find was not completely empty. "I was able to drive a good bargain for the two of them, so there's some money left there for you. I'll go and draw up the manumission papers now. You'll be needing those soon, I wager."

Calabar nodded slowly in gratitude and wonder and then turned back to face Affey, who could not restrain herself from asking another question. "He calls you Jupiter, as though he was your master. Why doesn't he call you by your right name?"

Calabar answered, surprised, "Why, I never did think to tell him my right name. Most everybody has been calling me Jupiter since I was freed." He frowned. "But you had more important questions that need answers first."

He led Affey over to his table and sat, waving a finger to summon the already clearly annoyed tavern keeper. The man scowled and came over, grumbling under his breath, "This is what comes of letting one blackbird under his roof – they will inevitably summon a whole flock."

Calabar fixed the man with a level, calm gaze and said, "This be my wife and baby, and they be freedmen like me today. Can we have two cups of cider while we talk?"

The tavern keeper grimaced and nodded curtly, moving back toward the bar, where he barked out to the tavern wench, "Missy, bring our guests their cider, and leave your young man alone for a bit."

Affey watched, her mouth agape. She said in a low voice, her tone one of amazement, "He is doing your bidding. The world is all kind of topsy-turvy now."

Calabar smiled and, after the tavern keeper sent his wench over with the ciders, began to explain how he had come to be in a partnership with Mister Cooper, and how that partnership had resulted in his relative affluence – and her release from service at the Greene plantation.

"Oh, Calabar, you would not believe how bad things have got back there. Cuffy's run off – "

"Run off?" Calabar's exclamation turned heads around the room, and he made a conciliatory gesture with his hands at those who were looking at him. In a quieter tone, he repeated, "Run off? What of his boy? And his woman, Mimba?"

"Master Greene whipped the boy something fierce, but he had nothing to tell the master. In the end, the sheriff brought him back around, after some local men found him in the woods by the crick."

She hesitated and then said very quietly, "As for Mimba, Master Greene took her for his bed, and he ain't given her back. Cuffy ran off because of it, but the master only flaunted it to us all the more after Cuffy came back."

Calabar shook his head sadly. "Cuffy never was one of the smart ones. Was he beaten badly?"

"Oh, he was a sight, and I had to use up so much of my supplies for poultices on him. Naturally, we have lots of tobacco about, but I ran plum out of comfrey and what all, so he moaned and carried on for days. Master Greene sold him, then, down to south, and without Mimba and their boy."

Calabar suppressed a gasp and shook his head sadly as Affey continued, "Old Hal finally went to his rest. Just didn't wake up one morning, but he looked at peace, so I'll shed no tears for him."

Calabar sighed and asked, "And what of the fields?"

"Oh, well, Master Greene, he told us to tear down all the vats, of course, and we had to build him up drying-houses for his tobacco. The fields have been dug up and made ready for planting his first crop of tobacco come springtime. Master seems to know what he's on about there, at least."

Calabar grimaced and nodded. "Mister Greene always did say that Master Green had a sound head for the business of tobacco."

Affey shook her head sadly. "Everything has been different since Mister Green died. First he sent you away, then the whole business with Cuffy, and tearing out your beautiful vats."

Calabar laughed bitterly. "I won't miss those vats – for the first time that I can remember, I feel like I've finally been able to wash the smell of them off of me. And if I ever get to feeling like I need to smell the indigo again, I can always go down to the market or the warehouse."

The tavern keeper approached their table again, looking more irritated than usual. "Man outside to see you, Jupiter."

"Can he not be come inside?"

Calabar saw the tavern keeper visibly master the urge to spit before he answered, "I don't let his kind through my doors." Calabar raised one eyebrow at the man. "Well, he's a blackbird like yourself, but he ain't a respectable sort," the tavern keeper explained.

Calabar stood and said to Affey, "You stay here. I'll see what this is about and come back." She nodded, frightened, but he could see the trust in her eyes.

He followed the tavern keeper out through the front door,

and was surprised to see Simbee waiting outside, although there was no sign of Little Pete. Simbee looked Calabar over, his face reflecting clear distaste for the freedman's adoption of Cooper's clothing style suggestions.

Simbee's soft voice was urgent and lower pitched than it had sounded before. "Little Pete been catch by sheriff. Need money for get him away. Come ask you, been ask others already."

Calabar closed his eyes and sighed heavily. "I spent my money already."

Simbee's eyes widened in surprise and disbelief, then narrowed in suspicion. "You been have too much money for spend so soon. You not want help Little Pete, just say."

Calabar prepared to launch into a lengthy explanation of how his fortune had been spent, but stopped himself. "It been my money. If I had it still, I been helping, but I used it for what I been needing." Simbee's eyes flashed with malice, but he said nothing. Calabar added, "How will money help Little Pete? Sheriff been saying that he sell back for slave any freedman he finds after one year."

"I buy him," the small man said simply. "He be my slave then, I take him secret plantation."

Calabar retorted, "Freedman can't be buying slave. And Little Pete be worth more than I be having anyway. And money I have, I be needing to find home for me, for my family."

"Can pay for buy," Simbee said stubbornly. "And when you got family?"

Calabar did explain then, laying out the whole story of how he had turned his fortune into the tool to bring his family back together.

Simbee had a faraway, thoughtful expression on his face as he pondered for a long moment before he spoke again. , "You can't be staying at tavern with woman and baby, be needing house somewhere else. Can sell house, sell more to other, get money for buy Little Pete."

It was Calabar's turn to be suspicious. "How you be having a house to sell?"

"Been building for live."

"Where is it? I be needing to stay near town for rest of my time, work with Mister Cooper."

"Near town, not in swamp."

"But you not be fearing sheriff find, catch you, too?"

Simbee shot him a baleful look. "Sheriff not be everywhere. House safe." His expression shifted, and he gave Calabar an appraising look. "Too much fear you. Should live."

Calabar suppressed the flash of anger that the smaller man's words kindled in his heart. Who was this man to lecture him on fear, all the while hiding off in a swampy settlement, while he himself stayed in town and found a means of improving his lot, dealing daily with the danger of living in town?

Still, Calabar had to admit, the prospect of a home for his family was an appealing one. "I do not be knowing how much money I have," he confessed, holding up his purse. "I have not been having any chance to count since Mister Cooper came back. What do you be needing?"

Simbee frowned. "Money be Little Pete's. I handle other thing."

Calabar opened his purse and felt about inside it. He recognized the heavy, reassuring shape of several guineas, with their grooved edges, along with a number of coins of lesser value. It was time for the student to become the teacher.

He pulled out a single guinea, and Simbee's eyes followed it avidly as he held it up. "This be a guinea. Twenty, thirty, maybe more, buy Little Pete."

He returned the coin to his purse and counted by feel. "I be having nine guineas still. Enough for to buy house from you?"

Simbee's eyes narrowed for a moment in thought and he nodded. "More be better, but you been buy two slave already today."

"Two freedmen," Calabar corrected him. "Mister Cooper be making sure of that right now."

"Mister Cooper buys Little Pete, too," Simbee said.

Calabar frowned and replied, "I not be knowing whether or not Mister Cooper be willing to do this again. But I will ask. How do I find the house I be buying from you?"

Simbee pointed down the road where it disappeared into the woods at the edge of town. "That way until cross two crick. Look for track under gum pine, this side" – the man patted his own left shoulder emphatically – "follow to big rock other side, go straight out pass rock, will see." He fell silent, seeming exhausted at having said so much in one stretch.

Calabar nodded solemnly and drew out the coins, one at a time, handing them over to Simbee. The smaller man accepted them, counting out as Calabar placed them in his hand, " . . . six, seven, eight, and nine." He closed his hand over the coins and nodded, satisfied. "Hope you like house. I build another for Little Pete, me."

Chapter 17

Calabar trudged down the road out of town beside Affey, who had Fantee strapped snugly on her back. They'd crossed over the first stream, passing by the fence lines of several plantations. Though Calabar carried their manumission papers tucked inside his waistcoat, they'd encountered nobody since leaving town.

A cold rain made the trip unpleasant for Calabar, but miserable for Affey and Fantee. The baby had been fussing for several miles now, and refused Affey's breast or other comforts. She was cold and miserable, and she was letting the world know it in no uncertain terms.

Although he knew that his heart ought to be soaring at his reunion with his family, and the fortuitous resolution of their housing problem, Calabar could not help feeling that this was not the way he'd pictured it. In addition to the challenges of the weather and the screaming baby, he was deeply irritated at the tavern keeper, who had steadfastly refused to return any of Calabar's money.

Calabar found the man's argument to be circular and unpersuasive. "You paid in advance, 'tis true, but it's none of my affair that you're choosing to depart before your time is up."

"Then I be staying, and my wife and baby be staying with me."

"You can have no more guests in the room without my

approval and payment of their room and board; I don't care to house any more blackbirds, so that's the end of the matter."

"So you be throwing me out, though my money be as good as any man's."

"Nay, you're welcome to stay on, though I am not inclined to continue our arrangement at the end of your paid-up time."

"And my wife and the baby? Where are they to stay?"

The tavern keeper shrugged. "Not my problem. They just can't stay here."

"Then I be wanting my money back for the time I not be using."

The tavern keeper crossed his arms over his chest, a self-satisfied smirk on his face. "I am afraid not, friend. Law's perfectly clear – I've no obligation to return your board, should you decide to leave before it's up. Sheriff will tell you, if you want to involve him."

From the way he said it, Calabar didn't doubt that this avenue of inquiry would end badly for him. In the end, he'd had to leave with his worldly goods stuffed into a rucksack, and no satisfaction from the tavern keeper.

Not knowing what awaited them at the house he'd bought, sight unseen, his first urge was to purchase the necessities to ensure that they'd be comfortable and well-fed, but Affey had convinced him to investigate the house first, and plan to come back to town to supplement any deficiencies.

He was starting to have serious doubts about that plan, as the miles passed by and the rain continued to fall. His stomach grumbled, and he knew that had he still been at the tavern, he would have had a warm meal waiting for him at his accustomed table, and the always cheerful Cooper for company.

Instead, the baby seemed to be giving voice to every complaint she'd had so far in her short life, all at once. Although Affey had covered her face against the rain with a flap of her sling, Fantee had pushed it aside, and was now irritably squalling into the drippy, chilly rain.

For her part, Affey walked with her shoulders back and her head up, the reality of her freedom evidently sinking in. Where Calabar was accustomed to seeing her with her head ducked down, trying to appear unobtrusive, she was now looking around as she walked, eagerly taking in the road ahead and their surroundings. She even exclaimed in delight as a deer erupted out of the woods on one side of the road just in front of them, leaping and flashing its white tail as it disappeared into the trees on the other side.

Calabar willed himself to share in her joy, but another great drop of water found its way under the brim of his hat and exploded across his face, making him scowl. Affey glanced back at him as he wiped the water from his cheek and nose. "I think that is the second crick up there."

She pointed past where the deer had disappeared into the woods, and Calabar could see where a small bridge had been erected to ford a brook that he could now hear babbling over the sound of rain dripping through the trees.

He felt his heart begin to race as they neared their newly purchased home. He had not devoted a lot of thought or curiosity to the question of what his land would look like, or how well the house would suit them, but now his pace quickened as he found himself eager to learn what he had purchased in exchange for the small handful of guineas he'd had left.

"And there's the gum pine Simbee told me to look for," he cried out gladly to Affey, striding forward and ahead of her toward it. At the tree, he turned to the left and saw a lightly traveled but muddy track leading away from the road, water puddled into a few footprints. He turned and took Affey's hand, leading her into the woods. She did not complain as mud squelched up between the toes of her unshod feet, but she did release his hand so that she could pick her way along the path more carefully than he was.

The rain had let up, but the water still dripped heavily from the dense growth overhead as they passed underneath. The path threaded in between huge trees, winding back and forth. In places, the undergrowth intruded upon it, and Calabar had to take care, lest a branch whip back and hit Affey, or worse, the baby, who had settled down somewhat with the end of the rain.

Finally, they came to a large outcropping on the right side of the track, and Calabar could see an even fainter track leading away. He gave Affey a tight, nervous smile and started down it.

A short way in, the woods opened up to reveal a clearing that backed up to a gentle hillside, with a small, rudely constructed cabin situated on a rise. Calabar's initial reaction was that it was ridiculously small for three people, and unbelievably primitive.

He looked back at Affey to apologize for his error in squandering so much of their remaining funds in buying such a home, and saw that her mouth hung open and her eyes were dancing with glee at the sight of the little cabin. Her delight forced him to look at the house in a different light, as he realized with a jolt that even this tiny structure was better built than their old slave quarters.

As he looked more closely at the house, he was gratified

to see that it was made from tightly fitted logs and roofed with shingles. He knew from experience what painstaking work went into splitting enough of those to cover a roof. The spaces between the logs of the walls were tightly packed with bark and dried mud, which would keep the wind out. At one end of the cabin, a rough but serviceable-looking chimney rose, promising warmth within.

A carefully built door hung on iron hinges – Calabar didn't want to guess how Simbee had acquired them – and was held snugly shut with a hand-carved latch. The house was situated on the rise in the center of the clearing such that the trickle of a creek that tumbled down the hillside behind it was guided naturally around to one side, keeping the house high and dry.

Affey touched Calabar's arm. "Can we go inside?" The baby had stopped fussing entirely and looked up at him expectantly, too, her dark eyes huge and solemn.

Calabar shook himself out of the reverie of examination of the exterior, answering, "Certainly. Let us see if it lives up to the promise of its fine appearance." He led the way up to the door and slid open the latch, pulling the door open.

Inside the cabin, there was little light, and the room smelled strongly of a man who did not care too much for frequent bathing mixed with the sharp reek of scorched meat and more than a little wood smoke. Affey entered behind Calabar, pausing beside him as they gave their eyes time to adjust to the darkness.

No window pierced the thick walls of the cabin, so the only light came from the doorway behind them. Calabar could see the hearth in the shadows, and thought he could perceive a small, neat stack of wood beside it.

Unlike the bright, windowed kitchen where Affey had

worked at the plantation, there was no collection of shining copper kettles, nor even heavy iron ones. No cooking cranes hung from the side of the hearth, ready to hold a pot and swing it to the perfect position over the coals. All that Calabar could see was a battered spider, standing unevenly on the swept floor before the hearth, Simbee's last meal before heading into town scorched into the bottom.

A sleeping pallet lay nearby, and Calabar sighed as he thought of his bed at the tavern. He comforted himself with the thought that at least he could build a version of that for himself readily enough. Now, though, they needed a fire to combat the afternoon's chill and ward off the cold of the night to come.

Calabar checked the hearth to see whether any coals still smoldered there, but found it as cold as the rain outside. This possibility, however, he was prepared for, and he rummaged through his pockets until he found the tinderbox he'd purchased before they left town. That much Affey had relented and suffered him to spend money on.

He knelt and started to clear the remnants of the old fire from the hearth so that he could lay a new fire, but Affey put her hand on his shoulder, saying, "You take Fantee and let me do this. I've much more experience at the hearth than you." He could not deny the truth of her statement, though it rankled him slightly to be relegated to dandling the baby while his wife labored at the hearth.

He stood and offered the tinderbox to her, though, and accepted the baby, who was now quietly taking in everything around her with wide, solemn eyes. Affey stacked wood in the hearth with practiced, efficient movements, and in no time she'd struck the flint and had the beginnings of a fire crackling and lighting the room.

As the fire began to climb up the wood Affey had laid in the hearth, and flames to leap upward toward the chimney, Calabar could see the source of the wood smoke smell in the room – the chimney leaked smoke in several places where there were gaps between poorly joined rocks. He noted it as something that would need attention, but he didn't know how to do the necessary work himself.

The rising light of the fire revealed the rest of the interior of the cabin, and Calabar was grateful to see that there didn't seem to be any places where the roof leaked. Though the sleeping pallet seemed to be the only furnishing in the room, there was a neatly stacked pile of Simbee's clothing along the far wall from the fireplace.

Carrying the baby around the room so that they could both inspect closely their new home, Calabar nodded to himself with satisfaction. With a little work, this was going to be a good place to live, a good place to raise a family. Looking at Affey, who still sat on her haunches tending the fire, Calabar realized that for the first time since the wretched interview with Master Greene that had ended with his abrupt freedom, he felt entirely at ease.

Chapter 18

Calabar rested against the rake he'd fashioned from a handily forked branch and a few other bits of whittled wood, surveying the small garden he and Affey had scraped out of the clearing over the winter months. The warmth of the early spring air gave him hope that they would be able to plant soon, trading hoarded cash for seeds in town.

The months since Affey's release had included the happiest days that Calabar could recall in his entire life, happier even than his cloudy memories of childhood back in the village, before he and his mother had been seized into slavery in the first place. It was enough that he was almost able to ignore events that would have previously left him gravely concerned.

The first few days had been challenging, it was true – he'd had to make the trek back into town several times to fetch food and other necessities, and to return Simbee's personal belongings. He'd learned from Simbee that while Cooper had been unable to prevail upon the sheriff to sell Little Pete to him, the money that Simbee had accumulated had been sufficient to pay a fine assessed by the sheriff.

That had earned Little Pete his release from custody, and the freedman had left the colony, promising never to return. "I be following him on morrow," Simbee had told Calabar, accepting the sack of clothing and tools gathered from the house. "This be no place for freedmen."

On Calabar's next trip into town a few days after that, he passed by a rough-looking crowd gathered around the broken and bleeding figure of a man, shouting encouragement to one another. Calabar could not honestly tell at first glance what sort of man was at the center of the crowd, but what clothing he had left intact looked much like the rags that Simbee had worn. He realized with a sick lurch of his stomach that his acquaintance had somehow failed to depart as planned.

"Reckon he's got the fight whipped out of him yet?" The familiar voice almost caused Calabar to stop and look to confirm that the speaker was in fact Master Greene. However, the crowd hadn't taken notice of him yet, and Calabar thought it likely that was for the best. He kept to the margins of the road, ducking his head down behind the cocked brim of his hat, just in case anyone saw him.

An answering voice called out over the shouts and jeers of the mob, "I don't suspect the sheriff will have to chase him back into the swamp now," and then, "Ho, there! I think I saw him reach for his walking cane, boys. Best keep him still to stop him from hurting any of us with it."

The sound of muffled blows and high-pitched shouts of encouragement were not enough to stifle a groan from their victim's throat, and Calabar burned with shame at the swift steps that carried him away from the scene of Simbee's torment.

A little closer to town, Calabar saw the sheriff hurrying down the road toward the scene of the crime, cursing and yelling to the mob. "That negro is no escaped slave - I saw his papers just yesterday! Mister Greene, I expect better of you!" Calabar was walking away too quickly to catch the rest of the exchange. Whatever justice the lawman might mete out, though, was likely to be too late for Simbee. This was, indeed, no place for freedmen.

Calabar had hurriedly finished his business in town, and had practically run back home, looking away as he passed the spot where the mob had done their foul business. At home, he'd said nothing of the matter to Affey, even though he could tell from her questioning glances that she knew that something was amiss.

Since that awful day, though, events had changed the balance of that consideration somewhat, in Calabar's opinion. While the conspiracy to move against the governor that Allbright had whispered to him about had failed to materialize, the sheriff had abruptly resigned, and was replaced with a man who seemed much more interested in ferreting out signs of rebellion and who quietly let it be known that he was not going to offer any rewards for the apprehension of freedmen who had overstayed their legal welcome in the colony.

Too, while Greene and his cronies had faced no charges for their cruel killing of Simbee, Cooper passed along to Calabar there had been talk for a while that they might be called to account for disturbing the peace, but nothing ever came of it. When Cooper gave him the update, he muttered to Calabar that he suspected that money had crossed the right palms, and that was that. Greene was appointed to lead the King's militia, though, which kept the man occupied with chasing rebels against the Crown, instead of supposed escaped slaves.

Calabar ventured to ask whether he thought that the district were likely to be safer for him and his family, now that the rowdiest elements around were focusing their efforts on chasing traitors.

"'Tis a rare wind that blows so ill that no good may come of it," Cooper agreed. "You are afforded some degre of safety, too, by the fact that you are already known about town as a freedman, and your manner of dress sets you apart from those who eke out their existence in the swamp. You may not have much in the way of rights, but you do have 'em."

Calabar nodded. "With Master Greene be looking for traitors, I be worried about Mister Allbright, though."

Cooper corrected him automatically, "I am worried about Mister Allbright," and then added, "I agree, but I do believe the old man can make account for himself, should it come to that."

Calabar still worried for the safety of his friend, but taking comfort from Cooper's reassurance, he had started to think unconsciously in terms of staying indefinitely in the little house he'd bought. The necessity of leaving before the summer was out no longer seemed as pressing, and he found that it altered his attitude and plans in subtle ways, as well as some that weren't so subtle.

He realized that he had set no departure plans in place when he started plotting out and turning earth for the garden plot. Other than a grimace to himself at the potential foolishness of doing so in such uncertain times, though, he dismissed the thought and continued finding ways to make their abode more comfortable.

On advice sought from Cooper, small stones that he found in the freshly exposed garden soil went into the chinks in the chimney, reducing the amount of smoke that leaked into the house. Affey had busied herself as well, cleaning the walls and smoothing the floors, to the point that Calabar could scarcely tell that they were only swept dirt. The clay-heavy soil, for all that it made the garden work heavy going, produced a solid and clean floor after

Affey was done with it.

Calabar had purchased a proper cooking kettle for Affey, and though she'd clucked at him over the expense, she had made heavy use of it since he'd brought it home. He'd kept it filled with rabbit and squirrel, trapped in the woods with snares he'd remembered how to make from his youth, supplemented with more purchases brought from town.

The most important of these were three hens and a loud, strutting rooster. The hens gave eggs, one or two per day between them, three on a couple of occasions. The rooster crowed on his own schedule – unlike the one at Greene's plantation which had waited until near the sunrise – and otherwise made a nuisance of himself, but, Calabar reminded himself, it would earn its keep come the spring, when it was time to let one of the hens go broody and raise the next generation of chicks.

To help him replenish his dwindling cash, Cooper had offered Calabar a few small jobs, assessing the quality of barrels for the upcoming season and the like, which had yielded some small income, but he knew that they would need to become self-sufficient as quickly as possible, before the money ran out entirely, and he was forced to return to doing errands about town. And so, the garden plot grew.

Fantee, too, was growing, standing and taking her first steps just a fortnight prior. She was a cheery presence, reflecting a house that often rang with laughter and joy. She was moving past babbling as well, and was already learning that when she asked for things by name, her mother and father were more likely to fetch them for her.

Affey adapted to her freedom with more flexibility than Calabar had been able to muster in the first months of his release from bondage, as she shifted from cooking and cleaning for a plantation house to managing just her own household. It was, he supposed, not that great a change in the daily routine, though the need to make her own decisions as to what needed doing next was a new challenge for her. More than once, Calabar had found her frowning intently into the fire, considering the range of options open to her.

However, her joy at being out from under the management of Master Greene, and at being with Calabar again, was without bound, and it came as little surprise to him when she had approached him a month ago as he labored in the woods, felling saplings to build a fence around the garden.

She touched his shoulder and he rose, after sticking the blade of his knife into the ground carefully. She embraced him and said quietly, "Calabar, I believe that we are going to have another baby."

He held her at arm's length, delight dancing across his face. "So soon?"

She looked to one side, smiling bashfully. "I am not surprised, Calabar." He grinned in reply, and drew her back into a tight hug.

After accepting his embrace for a long moment, she stepped back to look at him, a serious expression on her face. "How will we feed another babe?"

He shrugged. "I'll turn over more space for the garden." She fell back into his arms, and he could feel tears tricking down her face and onto his arm. He rubbed her back comfortingly and murmured quiet reassurances into her ear, "Everything is now as it ought to be, Affey. Another baby is wonderful news."

Chapter 19

The garden plot stretched in neat furrows, and he had brought bucket after laborious bucket filled with rich loam from the woods out to supplement the heavy soil in the clearing. He was confident that he and Affey would be able to raise ample food to take care of their burgeoning family, and was eager to see crops rising from the ground that were unambiguously his own.

It had been better than a week since the last frost, and he was confident that sprouts started now would find a welcoming spring season awaiting them. He scraped the rake over the last furrow one more time, breaking up a stubborn clod of soil, and then straightened, lifting the rake up to rest jauntily on his shoulder.

Standing the rake up beside his other tools by the door, he called inside through the open door, "Affey, I need to go into town to get seeds for the garden; there is no use in putting it off any longer." Fantee crawled enthusiastically out to the doorway, smiling to see him there. She sat up, and then pulled herself up on the doorframe, grinning and waving to him with her free hand.

Calabar grinned back at his daughter and stepped over to lift her up over his head, eliciting a thrilled giggle from the toddler. Affey came to the door then, a gentle smile on her face as she watched them play together.

"Do you mean to commit all of our remaining money to the

earth, then?"

Calabar put the baby down and turned to face his wife, his demeanor suddenly grave. "Perhaps not all of it, but the substantial portion, yes. Corn and yams, certainly. Beans. Greens, squash. I don't know what to expect to pay, but even if it comes as dear as the rest of what we have, then it will be worth it to feed us all this next year."

They'd had the same discussion a number of times as Calabar had prepared the garden space. Each time, it came down to a question of risk opposed to reward, and Calabar had come down every time on the side of risk. He knew that, should disaster strike and their garden fail utterly, there was an excellent prospect of being able to help Cooper with another crop of the indigo, and that this would restore his wealth in short order.

Affey, on the other hand, had argued consistently for caution. "You have no assurance that Mister Cooper will continue to require your help, nor even that the indigo will continue to move through the warehouses in town," she'd said the last time they'd discussed the matter. "Before I . . . left the plantation, I heard Master Greene's visitors discussing with him all manner of stories about the British closing ports, sending soldiers to these shores, and causing disruptions to the trade."

She'd looked frightened as she'd added, "I think that Master Greene was eager for the outbreak of open warfare, and his friends seemed to be excited for the coming opportunity to visit violence upon those whom they identified as enemies of the Crown."

In Calabar's mind, these factors argued even more forcefully for doing whatever they could to establish themselves as self-sufficient landholders, so that his family would no longer be dependent upon supplies from town to put food in their bellies. If one crop should fail, better to have others that might thrive.

He'd kept this reasoning to himself, though, only saying to Affey, "What I have learned in my brief time as a freedman is that there are always rumors of war, threats to peaceful life, but that the trade is rarely completely interrupted. It might be harder to secure particular items from time to time, but those sorts of disruptions do not even require war."

Now, he gave her a tight hug and said to her quietly, "My duty to you and to our children is to keep you safe and to provide for you; I believe that the best way to pursue these duties is to put our money into the ground, in expectation that we can turn it into food for us all." He held her at arm's length, smiling. "After all, we cannot eat half-crowns and tuppence."

She laughed faintly, agreeing. "I know, I know. Go, then, and bring back a little something for the baby, too."

He looked at her, surprised. "You don't want to come with me today?"

She said thoughtfully, "I hadn't made any plans to come along, but I see no reason to stay here alone." She fetched her sling and swung Fantee up into it, tucking her squirming arms and legs inside.

Fantee, for her part, was not in the mood to be carried and struggled for a bit, crying out, "Down! Down!"

Affey cuddled her close and offered her suck. "We have to go out, sweetie, and you can't keep up crawling." The baby accepted Affey's breast and quieted down, settling in to feed greedily. Affey smiled at her, and then turned to Calabar with a bright smile. "Let us be off, then."

The track to the main road was by now familiar, and Calabar greeted the landmarks with good cheer as they passed. Though the ground was soft with the spring rains, the last few days had been relatively dry, so it was not as muddy as on their first trip along it. Affey still lacked shoes, and Calabar secretly hoped that there might be enough money left over to stop by the cobbler's shop and correct that.

He'd already gotten her a small amount of cloth and sewing supplies, so that she could fashion a more suitable dress for herself, and had grand designs for a whole outfit for her and the baby with the next indigo season's proceeds. For the moment, though, Affey was content to walk, as she always had, on feet well-accustomed to making their way through the world without the benefit of shoes.

Once in town – quieter than its normal bustling state – Calabar decided to first pay a visit to his friend, the milliner. He felt guilty for how little time he'd given the man since Affey and Fantee's deliverance from slavery, and meant to correct that whenever possible, now that the heaviest work of making their new home suitable was complete.

As they moved through town, it seemed to Calabar that there were fewer people than normal out on the streets, and those people who were about were clustered in small groups, many of them appearing to be engaged in intense conversations. He was accustomed to being more or less ignored by most, but nobody, it seemed, had time for either a friendly greeting, nor even the occasional customary glare.

When they arrived at the milliner's shop, Calabar was unsurprised to see that the shutters and door were still closed up. He rapped at the door, fully expecting to have to rouse the old man from his slumber again.

To his surprise, however, he heard a whispered hiss through the door, "Who knocks? Thrice for liberty, once more for death!"

Confused, he answered, "It's just Jupiter, Mister Allbright. Is there something be wrong?"

There was a rasping noise, and the door cracked open just a bit. Calabar could see the milliner's good eye peering out, bright and alert for danger. The old man swung the door open and beckoned to Calabar. "Well, don't stand out there on the street. 'Tis unsafe, today of all days."

Puzzled, Calabar led Affey into the darkened shop, and the old man hurried to close the door up behind him, drawing a heavy bolt back across it to secure it. Calabar was surprised to note that a musket stood beside the doorway, clearly ready for use if needed. "Why are you alarmed so, Mister Allbright?"

Calabar could just make out Allbright's grimace in the gloom. "The Committee has moved against the royal governor this very day, and his militias are abroad all across the colony, seeking those upon whom they can fix the blame, and those who can be made to answer for the insults to their sovereign. I had no part in this plot, but I am well-enough known from my days amongst the Regulators that I should be surprised only if I do not fall under suspicion before nightfall."

Affey gasped behind him, and Calabar felt an icy clutch of fear in his heart on his old friend's behalf. "Would they hurt you, just for they think you were involved?"

The old man nodded sharply. "They would not hesitate to do so," he said with a heavy certainty. "Those who remain loyal to the Crown and to the person of its governor in this colony are eager to find someone upon whom they can visit their anger for the fact that their man was forced from his fine Government House – yes, the selfsame one the construction of which brought the Regulators to the field so many years ago, and in opposition to the which I sacrificed my eye – and an old, half-blinded man makes an easy target."

He nodded in the direction of the gun. "Not so easy as they may think, though. I may not sleep again on this side of the grave, but if they will help me along, I shall not go to my rest alone."

"Was the governor hurt, then?"

"Nay, not that I've yet heard, but he has flown, and I do not doubt that he is pursued by some who have no gentle intentions for him."

Affey asked querulously, "Be we safe here?"

Allbright turned to her, and Calabar could see even in the little light that penetrated the shutters that his face was lined with care and sadness. "Nay, 'tis not likely a safe place for a woman and babe." He turned back to face Calabar, adding, "Nor for a freedman already associated with helping an escaped slave slip through the fingers of the sheriff."

Again Affey gasped. "How is that? Calabar, what have you done?"

She covered her mouth as Allbright's face registered puzzlement. The old man said slowly, "Calabar?"

Calabar interjected, "Mister Allbright, my true name be Calabar, but I been called Jupiter by my master for so long that it make no difference to me." Answering Affey, he said, "I have not been knowing that Little Pete was escaped. He always done said he was freed, and the sheriff not been knowing either, else he would never been release Little Pete."

He shrugged. "Little Pete been friend, so even if I been knowing, I been help Simbee." He smiled and added, "We got house for trouble."

Allbright said, "Jup-, I mean, 'Calabar,' your dear Anna has the right of it. You ought leave now, and no matter the urgency of your errand in town today, you should return to your home and sit behind a barred door for the next day or two, just in case someone decides to visit mischief upon the countryside. All those under arms are aswarm today, and even friends cannot be relied upon to ensure your safety."

Calabar made a sour face at the prospect of abandoning his friend to the fates, but the fear in Affey's eyes as she clutched the baby made up his mind. He nodded.

"Be safe, friend of mine," he said, tipping his hat. "Be you not too eager to see your rest today. I be looking forward to be talk much more with you still."

The old man nodded in acknowledgement and slid back the bolt on his door. "Travel safe and travel swift; get yourselves off the roads as quickly as ever you can."

The pair slipped out of the shop and the old man closed the door firmly behind them, the bolt rasping in its hasp a final time behind them. Affey needed no encouragement to hurry away and back toward the road to their house, and Calabar had to lengthen his stride to keep pace with her.

They were at the outskirts of town when the worst came to pass. Toward them down the wooded road came marching a squad of men, muskets shouldered but primed. Though they wore no uniform, their haughty bearing and stormy expressions revealed in an instant that they were a loyalist militia, and Calabar felt shock steal over his body in a chill as he spied Master Greene at the head of the column, his eyes flashing at the sight of the three freedmen.

Holding a hand up to motion the other men to a standstill, he accosted Calabar with a glare. "Where do you suppose you are going in the company of these runaways?"

Calabar protested, fighting to overcome the feeling of being hopelessly tongue-tied. "They not be runaways. They be freed, same as me. Better." He reached into his waistcoat to retrieve the manumission papers, and was shocked to see Greene level his weapon on him.

He stared down the cavernous bore of the musket, keenly aware that his death rested at the bottom of the barrel. Looking back up to Greene's face, he was almost as shocked to see terror in the other man's eyes.

Greene swallowed hard, glanced around him at the other militiamen, and barked, "You had better not have a pistol in there, boy! I know that these two are runaways, as I just sold them off this very year."

"No, sir, I been getting out our manumission papers." Calabar hated to hear the quaver in his own voice, but with the muzzle of the gun still dark and ominous in front of his eyes, it was all he could do to speak at all.

Greene nodded curtly and lowered his gun slightly. Then, looking at Calabar more closely, his eyes narrowed in suspicion, and he raised it again. "Ain't you the negro I sent away after the last harvest?"

Calabar gulped and answered, "Yes, sir."

"And where did you steal such fine clothes, boy? You ain't

had a pot to spit in when you left, and I know for a fact that you ain't had any worthwhile skills by which to support yourself."

Calabar's shoulders slumped at the impossibility of explaining his good fortune to the man who'd found him not worth even trying to sell at auction. "I been working for a merchant," he offered, reluctant to expose Greene's foolishness while the man still held a weapon trained on him.

Greene raised an eyebrow and said sardonically, "More likely you've done robbed a merchant." He turned to the militiaman behind him, a corpulent, short man, with a ruddy, moist face. "What should I do with this negro who done stole fine clothing from a citizen?"

The shorter man said hesitantly, "Bring him to the sheriff?"

Greene made a show of pondering the man's advice, and finally nodded. "That's a fine idea, though not so much entertainment as I'd thought to get out of him. And what about the woman?"

Calabar could feel Affey tense up, and he pulled her behind him to shield her from whatever vile intentions might be stirring in the minds of their tormentors.

The shorter man seemed on surer ground when he answered this time. "We should bring her to the sheriff as well, and get the reward for capturing her for stealing herself away." He looked thoughtful for a moment, and then added, "Of course, the reward may be for turning in this fellow, both for robbing the merchant and for stealing the woman."

"That there is what we call solid thinking," Greene said, and prodded Calabar in the shoulder with the muzzle of his musket.

"Turn around and let me bind your hands, so that you can't get into any mischief while we escort you in to justice."

Calabar could see no choice, and he turned, facing Affey. She looked into his eyes for the space of two heartbeats, her expression filled with terror, and then she turned and fled, clutching the baby close to her as she ran.

Greene cursed, and Calabar felt the pit of his stomach fall into the earth as the air behind his ear was rent with the clap of a musket blast. Affey kept running, though, and Greene shouted to one of the militiamen behind him to catch her. The young man sprinted after Affey, disappearing into the woods behind her.

As he watched the pursuit, his heart pounding in his throat, Calabar heard a sudden rush behind him, and then he was falling to the ground, and in a moment, all was dark confusion.

Chapter 20

After what seemed like days of jostling and the sounds of distant argument, Calabar became aware of someone draping a wet cloth across his forehead. He groaned, and was surprised to see the grim face of a man – the new sheriff – swim into view over him. "You're hurt, boy, but you'll get better. Not so sure about your woman – she's in a bad way. Baby's fine, though. I've got a girl from my house caring for her."

Calabar started to sit up in reaction to the man's words, but the pain that shot through his whole head forced him back to the pallet where he'd been placed. "Rest easy, boy. I've sent for a surgeon to physic your woman." His grimace deepened. "My expense under the law, though I'll likely take it out of those overeager King's men who brought the three of you in."

"How – how they been hurt my Affey?" In his pain and confusion, Calabar could scarcely form words at all, and forgot entirely to use her slave name.

The sheriff gave no indication that he was aware of either error, answering only, "She ran off, and they were none too gentle in bringing her back in. Her face is busted up, and she got kicked in the belly pretty good, judging from boot mark on her clothes, and she appears to be bleeding from – well, she's bleeding, so I'm going to have her physicked proper."

"Where is she?" Calabar could hear the fear and pain in his

own voice, and a part of him cringed to know how much of his heart he was exposing to the lawman.

"Just in the next room. Sleeping right now, which is a mercy, if you ask me."

Calabar closed his eyes tightly to try to hold in the tears that he felt spring into them. Finally, without opening them, he asked, "What will become of us?"

"You?" The sheriff seemed genuinely surprised at the question. "Why, your papers are all in order, and you've been freed for these past few months, so you are free to go as soon as you are healed enough. Them boys had no business roughing you up, and no cause at all to bring you into custody. I gave them a good talking to, and they won't bother you anymore."

Calabar was mildly surprised that the sheriff didn't add a warning about his six months nearly being up. He wondered whether there was a change in the law, or its interpretation under this sheriff, but he didn't ponder the matter for very long. He had other, more pressing concerns.

He opened his eyes again and sat up, more gingerly this time. "I be wanting to see my wife," he said, with more firmness of purpose than he felt. In truth, the last thing he wanted to see was how badly Affey was hurt, but he knew that she needed him by her side right now.

As he slowly got to his feet, the sheriff stood by, his arms crossed over his chest and his grim expression relieved only slightly by a hint of compassion in his eyes. Calabar took a deep breath and asked, "Which way, sir?"

The sheriff uncrossed his arms and waved at the doorway. Calabar shuffled through, and the other man followed him without saying a word. The next room was brighter than the one where Calabar had been placed, and Calabar had to restrain himself from crying out aloud at seeing Affey.

She had been laid on a proper bed, and one side of her face was swollen almost beyond recognition. Dried blood was crusted all along a gash on her cheek, and where it had dripped down and pooled in the delicate whorl of her ear. Her mouth lay agape, and he could see that she'd lost at least two teeth to the beating, along with whatever physical insults she'd suffered elsewhere.

Calabar did not even try to contain his tears now, sinking to the floor beside her bed and weeping openly. She stirred at the sound, and her hand stroked the top of his head. "Calabar," she said indistinctly, and her hand fell back to the bed.

He did not reply, but took her hand in his, pressing it to his lips and sobbing over it. He heard some movement behind him, and the sheriff put a surprisingly gentle hand on his shoulder. "Doctor's here, boy. You can come out and wait outside with me."

Calabar kissed Affey's warm hand again and laid it across her chest as he stood, blinded by his tears, and followed the other man out into the sunlight. The doctor, an indistinct small form, hurried past and closed the door behind himself.

The sheriff guided Calabar to a pair of chairs at the front of the building. "Sit," he said gruffly. "Doctor's a proper surgeon and apothecary. If your wife can be healed, he will do it."

A bell began tolling an alarm in the distance, and the sheriff spat out a curse as he stood, adding, "What more can this day bring?" He stepped out into the street to see what the fuss was about and cursed again. "There's a house afire. I'd best go and help; you'll be all right if you just stay here."

He stepped back to the side of the building, and by the time he emerged, holding a pair of heavy gloves, a man was running wildly toward him, shouting, "The King's men have gone and fired the old man's shop, and him still inside it!"

Calabar started at the man's words, rising and calling back, "What old man be you meaning?"

The man seemed to be startled to hear a question from Calabar, but recovered himself, answering, "That crazy old hat-maker, Allbright. They caught him with proof that he'd been a part of the plot against the governor, and took the law into their own hands."

As Calabar felt his blood run cold, the sheriff shot him a knowing glance. "I've heard tell that he is a friend to you, boy, but you've got to stay here and tend to your wife when the doctor's done with her. I'll see to this . . . but the old coot has a history, and it wouldn't surprise me in the least if he were guilty of everything the mob – excuse me, the King's militia – says."

He grimaced, his face seeming to be accustomed now to the expression. "They should have brought him to me for justice, but the result would have been the same in the end." He pointed at the chair behind Calabar firmly. "You sit, and keep yourself out of this."

Calabar sat, feeling numb. He knew that Allbright would have given no quarter to the marauding squad of loyal militiamen, and he knew all too well that the old man likely had been involved, to one degree or another, in the unrest.

His own disaster seemed distant already in comparison to the awful fate that seemed to have overcome his friend. Fresh tears stung his eyes, and he wiped them away angrily. He could not help but hope that the old man had made good on his determination to bring along a set of King's men to escort him into the hereafter.

He heard Affey cry out, and found himself through the door and at her side, almost without conscious thought. The doctor looked up sharply at him, one hand on her belly and the other out of view under her blanket.

"You ought wait outside," he said, his voice harsh and cold. "I don't need you here while I see to this negress."

"Maybe not, but my wife be needing me, and I be staying." Calabar took Affey's hand again, and scowled resolutely at the small man. He noticed that the doctor's face was pockmarked and that a bead of sweat sprang up on his forehead, despite the spring chill that lingered in the air.

The little man broke his gaze away from Calabar's eyes and shook his head, his mouth pursed into an expression of frustrated disapproval. Calabar held his scowl for an instant longer, until Affey whimpered again and clutched at his hand. Calabar looked at her face then, and found the eye that wasn't swollen shut fixed on him.

Again, she simply said, "Calabar," and this time squeezed his hand in emphasis, her good eye never leaving his face.

"I be here, Affey," he said quietly. "He just be trying to see how badly hurt you be."

"Where is Fantee?" Her eye held fear now, and Calabar gave her hand a reassuring stroke with his thumb.

"Sheriff tells me she be fine, with a girl at his house."

"The baby?" She motioned with her eye at the doctor.

The surgeon's mouth was still set in a firm line when Calabar turned to look at him. The little man only shook his head once, saying, "If she was pregnant, she is no longer. I am no midwife, but she is bleeding more heavily than even a woman freshly delivered of child would."

Affey sank back onto the bed, her eyes closed, and Calabar fell to his knees beside her, sharing in her grief at this fresh loss.

The surgeon withdrew his hands and stepped back, his manner brisk. "I can see no reason that you should not recover from your injuries sufficiently to return to your labors. Your face will heal, and I wouldn't ordinarily waste it on the likes of you, but the Sheriff says you're to be treated, so I will leave you with a little bit of laudanum to dull the pain for a while. Your arm is badly bruised, but the bones do not appear to be broken, nor have you any lasting damage to your face, aside from a couple of teeth that look to have been freshly lost."

He shook his head. "I cannot tell if you can again bear children, but time will tell. You were lucky not to have been hurt worse, given that you ran from men who were but executing their duties to King and country."

Calabar stood, a stormy scowl coming over his face. "We be freedmen," he said quietly. "They been having no business chase us to start with."

The doctor made a sour expression. "Freedmen or no, there was no need to run and provoke them. They were within their rights to bring you to the sheriff, and let him decide your status." He looked at the two of them thoughtfully. "Were I you, I would leave this colony for some happier place, or seek my fortune among my own kind."

He shrugged, gathering up his things. "It's none of my affair, though. I hope that the morrow gives you comfort and an improvement to your disposition." He bustled past them and closed the door firmly behind him.

After he'd left, Calabar sank back down beside the bed, all of his strength now gone. He felt Affey's quaking sobs echoing his own, and through their tears, he wondered if the world would ever again feel as full of promise as it had that morning.

Chapter 21

Calabar felt as though he were drained of all the tears that his eyes could ever produce, and was just sitting beside Affey, summoning the strength to keep breathing as an act of will. She had returned to the blessed sanctuary of sleep, and he was taking comfort in watching her breathe, his own chest rising and falling in unconscious synchrony to hers.

He startled at the sound of a knock, and was relieved to hear Mister Cooper's familiar voice calling in through the door, "Are you in there, Jupiter?"

Calabar found that he could stand up, and took a deep, shuddering breath before answering, "Yes, Mister Cooper, I be here." Cooper opened the door and slipped in, looking slightly furtive as he closed the door behind himself.

"I'd heard that you might be here, and I have learned, too, of the terrible events of the day." Calabar could smell smoke and wondered whether it was in the air that had come in with the merchant – or was it on his clothes? Instead of making him think of warmth and cheer, it reminded him of the suffering and death that the day had visited upon his family and his friend.

Cooper stood before him, turning his hat nervously about in his hands and looking anxiously past Calabar at Affey. "Will Anna be all right? And your daughter?"

Calabar nodded, barely trusting himself to speak. "Little

Fantee was not hurt, the sheriff been told me. But our next baby been killed up in her belly." He was only slightly surprised to note that his eyes could still well up with more tears.

He was more surprised to see tears spring up in Cooper's eyes, too, as the man rushed forward to take his hand, exclaiming, "I am so very sorry to hear of this loss imposed upon you!" Calabar stood awkwardly, unsure of what to say in reply, until the other man dropped his hand and stepped back, looking abashed.

"Was it, as I have heard, the King's militia, who abused you and your wife so?"

Calabar nodded again. "Master Greene been thinking that Anna been a runaway, and that I been a thief." He gestured at his clothes, noticing for the first time that one knee of his trousers was ripped out, and that he was covered in dirt.

He chuckled ruefully, adding, "Nobody be thinking that I stole these now, I guess." Overcome again, his chin dropped to his chest as he attempted to gather himself. Cooper had seen him lower, but he didn't want to exhibit so much weakness before his friend, regardless.

"What might you say, Mister Jupiter, were I to suggest that there might be a way for you to help ensure that such injustices are not visited upon your family again, nor upon other innocents in this colony?"

Calabar looked up, confused. "How can I do such a thing? I just be one man, and a negro at that."

Cooper glanced about the room, as though he expected that they might suddenly have been joined by some other person. "I've chosen a side, is how. Our Committee of Safety is taking up arms in the wake of Mister Allbright's murder, and all freedmen are welcome to join us."

Calabar was so surprised at the revelation that he actually took a step back to stand in stunned silence while Cooper held his gaze, his expression serious and sympathetic.

"I have no arms to be taken up," Calabar said eventually. "I have never been learning any useful arts of violence. What sort of soldier could I be?"

Cooper nodded, his eyes still grave. "Muskets we have, though we would need to teach you their use. I will not dissemble with you; most of what the freedmen in our company have been called upon to do is the sort of brute labor that they did while they were bound to service. I know full well that your greatest gifts are anything but warlike, yet I felt compelled to offer you the chance to avenge the violence you have suffered, while performing a service to others in a like situation."

He raised his hand in dismissal, saying, "We should speak no more of these matters in this place, however. There is no need to make any commitment in this moment, either. There will be time for all of this talk later."

He glanced around the room again, registering for the first time that it was the county gaol, though he said nothing to Calabar. "I know that you have established your own home, but I mistrust the safety of travel anywhere on this day of mayhem and death. Where is your daughter, anyway?"

Calabar explained what the sheriff had told him, and Cooper said, "We shall need to send for her, then. Is your Anna in any condition to move?"

"I be thinking that she should not be moved until the surgeon says that she is strong enough."

Cooper nodded sharply, his brow beetled in concern. "I am sure that you are wise in this, yet I wish we could keep her in a place away from the militia that brought you here in such condition." He shook his head, adding, "What cannot be changed, though, we must accept as it is. I should not stay any longer, in any event. When Anna is well enough that you may leave her side, come and find me at the tavern."

After Cooper left, the turmoil in Calabar's head seemed only to add to the throbbing ache that had been his companion ever since he'd awoken here. He returned to Affey's side, his mind awhirl with the surprising – and dangerous – opportunity that Cooper had laid before him.

It had honestly not even occurred to him to consider returning the violence that had been committed against Affey and himself. The militiamen were white, landowners, and well-respected in the community. A freedman, living in a precarious state within the colony, and a freeholder only by virtue of his presence on the land, his first impulse was to avoid any potential conflict, not seek it out.

On the other hand, a sputtering flame of anger burned in his heart at the harm done to his wife and their baby, and the chance to indulge in some act of vengeance against those who'd unjustly attacked them appealed to that nascent rage.

He realized, too, that there was a deep appeal to Cooper's suggestion that he could help prevent such horrors from visiting others who were guilty of nothing more than being in the wrong place when the King's men happened along.

Affey turned in her sleep and groaned, her swollen cheek temporarily masking the beauty he knew was there, and he wept anew at the fact that he had not been able to protect her or their baby. It was in that moment that he knew that he would take up Cooper's offer, and learn the wholly foreign trade of warcraft.

Chapter 22

"We ain't got enough of these to go around, but this here's the most common musket you'll likely see. They're all come from the smithies back in the mother country, and the King's own issue them out to both militia and regular companies alike, for uniformity, right?"

Calabar was less than comfortable with the weapon sitting on the bench, given that the last time he'd seen one like it, he had been staring down the bore. However, with Affey settled more or less comfortably with Fantee at the tavern after the surgeon had declared her fit to move – in Calabar's old room, the tavern keeper having scowled deeply, but overcoming his qualms about housing more "blackbirds" with the aid of Cooper's purse and a few sharp words from Cooper – the merchant had brought him to the gunsmith's house to give him a basic understanding of the sorts of guns he might expect to handle and work with, should he agree to take up with the militia.

Most of the men who signed up with the militia had grown up using guns, and many already owned their own weapons, but Cooper knew that Calabar's past would only have introduced him to firearms from the point of view of a potential target, not a wielder.

On meeting him, the gunsmith had looked him up and down and remarked only, "Friend of Allbright's? Friend of mine, then. Name's Phillips. You look to be tall enough for a musket, or, if we can find you one and it suits you, even a rifle. We'll see what providence supplies."

Now he was going over the different parts of the weapon, and Calabar was working on overcoming his aversion to the infernal device, as well as trying to put aside for the moment the worries over Affey's recovery from the attack. The realization that he might soon carry and even use the same sort of instrument that had been used to menace him was a sobering one, and it concentrated his attention tremendously.

Phillips pointed to the wooden part of the gun. "That's the stock. Goes up on your shoulder, nice and firm, so that it doesn't jump about too much when you fire." He hoisted the gun up to his own shoulder, illustrating.

Calabar noticed that his hand fell naturally over the mechanism, and Phillips, seeing Calabar's glance at his hand, said, "Yep, that's the trigger. You notice that I don't put my hand inside the guard – that little cage around it – unless I am ready to shoot the gun. You'll see, too, that even though I haven't yet prepared the gun to fire, I never point it at anything that I am not willing to put a hole into."

He set the gun back down and gestured at part of the mechanism that held what appeared to be a chip of rock. "This here is the flint. When I pull the trigger, that releases the hammer, letting the spring that pulls the flint down to the frizzen, where it will strike a spark, just like the one you use to light your hearth." The frizzen he'd pointed at was a plate that stuck up from the top of the gun, leaning forward as though avoiding the flint.

Phillips pulled back on the piece holding the flint – the

hammer, Calabar reminded himself – until an audible click could be heard, and continued his explanation. "I'm not going to load the gun right now, because powder is dear under the current trade disruptions and, more importantly, because I don't want to shoot it inside here, but this is how you'd start. Later on, we will spare the powder to go out into the woods and fire a shot or two, just so that you know what to expect of it."

Calabar was intrigued to see that as Phillips pulled the trigger back, the plate – the frizzen – followed it back, standing up almost perpendicular from the top of the gun now. "If you're on the field of battle, you'll have prepared cartridges containing the right amount of charge, as well as your ball, but you can also prime and load your gun the old way, from a horn. In either case, you'll put a little bit of the powder here" – he pointed at a small dish that sat under the frizzen – "after you've loaded your charge." He pushed the frizzen closed, so that it covered the pan, remarking, "Don't want your powder to all pour out through the touch-hole."

He lifted the gun from the bench, set the stock down on the floor, and pantomimed pouring powder down the barrel. "So, your powder goes in first, setting aside a little bit for the pan. Then you'll wrap your ball in some paper or cloth, just enough so that it will seal against the walls of the bore, and use the ram to tamp it down nice and snug. Have a care, though, because you don't want to take any chances of striking a spark and setting off the charge while you're ramming it."

He set the gun back up on the bench and pushed the frizzen forward, fully exposing the small dish under it. "This is the pan. You'll put the rest of the charge in there, snap the frizzen back in to place, and then finish cocking, and finally, aim and fire." He demonstrated, pulling the hammer back until a second click was heard, and then again hoisted the gun to his shoulder, sighting down the barrel at the wall.

He gave a wry smile. "Do not worry overmuch about aiming. The Bess is a wondrous reliable weapon, but she's no rifle. A well-trained gunner can load and fire as much as five times in a single minute; only a higher rate of fire ensures that the enemy's line is struck more quickly than your own. If you're on a line, though, you'll load by command, in time with your fellows on the line, and that will slow you down somewhat."

He pulled the trigger, and the hammer fell with a loud snap and a bright spark, startling Calabar. He shot Phillips a nervous grin, and the other man grinned in reply, setting the gun down. "Shouldn't have done that," he said, his tone apologetic. "But 'tis good for you to get some sense of how the action of the thing operates."

He produced a small whisk on a chain with a pin dangling from the other end, holding it up for Calabar to examine. He then opened the frizzen, saying, "After you've fired a live round, you'll want to clear the pan, and ensure that the touch-hole is clear." He whisked out the pan and ran the pin through the touch-hole, pointing it out to Calabar.

"If that gets fouled up, the charge in the pan may go off true, but the flame can't reach the main charge, and your load will hang fire." He grimaced, adding, "I've known men who tried to clear a hang fire and lost fingers or worse when the cursed thing went off."

He stepped back, waving at the gun with his hand and saying, "Now you show me how you'd go about loading and handling the thing."

Calabar took a deep breath and stepped forward. Hesitantly, he lifted the gun from the bench, aware of Phillips' eyes on him. He pulled back the hammer, watching the action of the mechanism, and feeling the click as it reached loading position.

Somehow, the solid, certain feeling of the unseen parts inside the gun lent him confidence. These parts were meant to move in a particular manner, predictable and reliable, and all he had to do was to play his part in the operation of the device. He remembered the rickety mechanism he and his crew had worked on to stir the indigo, and the contrast between how that device felt under his hands and how this one felt made him feel like he could trust it even more.

As he had seen Phillips do, he set the butt of the gun down onto the ground and said, "Now I be putting in the powder, and wrapping the ball." Phillips nodded, and Calabar drew the tamping rod out of its socket and pushed it down the barrel, as though a real charge and bullet lay within. He slid the rod back into its place, and lifted the gun back up to the bench. He tipped up the frizzen to mime loading the pan, let it snap back into place, and pulled the hammer back until he felt the second click, even more satisfying than the first.

Phillips just grinned at him, speechless for a moment. "You look as though you've been doing that all your life, friend. You got a natural gift for machines?"

Calabar shrugged, remembering again the complex mechanism of the indigo paddles. "I been having not many machines to work with before."

Phillips nodded. "I suppose you ain't. I confess that I am eager to see how you fare with real powder and ball. Would you care to venture out with me to a good spot I know?"

Calabar frowned. "I been knocked about by the King's militia just yesterday. Be we safe?"

Phillips scowled in answer. "I heard all about the violent acts of the King's men yesterday, and the harm that you and your wife came to at their hands. After showing their bravery by beating a couple of freedmen and burning an old man in his shop yesterday, the lot of them are today sleeping off the rum they drunk to celebrate with."

He spat. "I'll tell you true, I might hope that some of them show their faces today, while we are armed. I only wish that poor old Allbright had not been taken by surprise, else he might have laid low some of those who took his life."

Calabar felt a stab of sorrow at the mention of the old milliner's name, and was saddened even further at the news that Allbright's last wishes had not come to pass. It seemed to him that the very least that a just world could have given the old man was the chance to avenge himself. He nodded to Phillips. "I be liking that, too."

Phillips' mouth quirked into a brief smile as he took the musket from Calabar and carefully uncocked it; Calabar watched closely, noting how he held the hammer back with a thumb, pulled back the trigger and then lowered the hammer slowly. "We will put that hope to good use, friend, but we must first attend to thoroughly acquainting you with the tools by which you may do so."

Calabar smiled grimly in reply. "I be glad to learn now."

The woods outside of town felt less welcoming to Calabar than they had before the attack. Now, instead of peering ahead to see what new landmark or wild animal he might be able to spot, he found himself looking around nervously, his glance darting from one shadow to the next, watching for any hint of human movement.

Beside him, Phillips was also alert, but it was clear that this was just his normal state of mind in the woods. Somehow, he made it look more relaxed, though he was just as quick as Calabar to spot the source of a rustle in the leaves, or the sound of a twig snapping.

The flintlock was slung over Phillips' shoulder, and he carried a cartridge case at his waist. Before they'd left, he had walked Calabar through the process of preparing paper cartridges. "Not much worth doing when you're just hunting, but if your quarry might shoot back, the seconds you save with a prepared cartridge could mean the difference between you and the other fellow going home."

Calabar nodded somberly, knowing that if the time came, he was unlikely to have the edge in experience. He hoped, though, that he might be able to make up for it in part by attending closely the lessons that Phillips offered – both the formal ones that he spoke aloud, and the more important ones that Calabar was soaking up by watching his every move.

For his part, Phillips seemed to be aware that his student was absorbing more than just the things he said by rote, and so he narrated his actions as he loaded the cartridges, slung the gun, and walked along, pointing out tidbits as he did so.

"You'll see that there's a socket here at the front of the gun. That's for a bayonet, which is a sort of spear point that attaches to the gun. I haven't got one of those – they're usually issued to soldiers, and by the time I came into possession of this particular weapon, the bayonet had been taken off for some other purpose."

Calabar had noted this comment, filing away in his mind the

point that this made the Brown Bess into a spear that could fire a bullet – a handy combination, particularly under the circumstances of British interference with shipping that Phillips had mentioned. Calabar thought it hardly a mere happenstance that warlike supplies like gunpowder should be difficult to secure.

Finally, after they'd left the road behind and tromped through the woods for some time, following a track that only he could see, Phillips called out to Calabar, "Here's the place. Good hill there, and nothing beyond it other than some Indians maybe, and if we was to accidentally hit one of them, it would only clear the way for another farmer out here."

He winked, adding, "Not too many of 'em left, though. Most hied off north after a war betwixt the tribes back in my granddaddy's day."

Calabar frowned, but kept his thoughts to himself. He knew that there were more than just Indians in these woods, and wondered whether the gunsmith would be so casual about an accident involving a freedman – or even a runaway – like himself or Simbee.

He was diverted from these bitter thoughts, though, as Phillips unslung the Bess from his shoulder and began to load it, his motions practiced and smooth. Within seconds, the man dropped to one knee, lifted the gun to his shoulder and fired.

Even though he knew that it would be loud, the sound caught Calabar unprepared for just how the report actually was. He jumped in spite of himself, and as the cloud of smoke cleared around Phillips' shoulders, he saw that the man was grinning.

"You ready to take a turn at it?" He stood and held the weapon out to Calabar. Calabar accepted it, holding it up to see how the frizzen, hammer, and pan were all situated now that the gun had actually been fired.

Carefully lowering it so that it pointed down toward the ground, he peered toward the hill. "I been too surprise to see where the shot been gone," he commented, pointing in the direction where Phillips had fired.

"I was aiming for that tree, about a hundred paces out." He pointed at an oak tree with a wide trunk, pockmarked with the results of earlier practice sessions. He shrugged. "Didn't hit it, and I suppose that my ball is buried somewhere back in the hill there, along with many others. One day, if lead becomes hard to come by, I might come out and do some mining." He grinned, and Calabar couldn't help but return his smile.

Phillips opened the flap covering the cartridges in his case and pulled one out, handing it to Calabar. "Go ahead; I believe that you know what to do."

Calabar accepted the cartridge, going through the process of loading the gun slowly and methodically for this first time. Later, he told himself, he'd worry about speed. For now, he just wanted to get it right.

Once the tamping rod was back in place, he lifted the weapon to his shoulder and finished cocking it. He sighted down the barrel toward the oak, slipped his finger inside the guard to find the trigger itself, and pulled it, feeling the tension inside the device resist him.

When the shot went off beside his ear, he thought for a moment that he might have deafened himself for good. His headache, which had receded since the prior day, came back with splitting intensity, and it was all he could do to not drop the gun as it leapt upward in his grasp.

When he lowered the weapon, Phillips was nodding in approval. "Most kids, first time they fire a gun, they holler and fuss, and a lot of them throw the thing away from themselves. Not only that, but you hit the tree with your very first shot."

Calabar looked again at the tree, and saw a fresh scar on its trunk, a spot of shattered bark revealing a bit of the lighter interior of the tree. Despite the pain in his head, he found himself grinning from ear to ear.

"Want to try another?" Phillips was already opening his cartridge case and drawing out a second cartridge to hand to Calabar. The freedman nodded eagerly, taking the neat paper bundle from Phillips' outstretched palm.

This time, he loaded the shot more quickly, feeling a bit more confident that he understood how all of the parts needed to go together. Again, he aimed for the oak, targeting the place where the first shot had left a bright circle of blasted bark. After the smoke cleared, there was a fresh scar on the tree, not more than a hand's breadth away from the first.

Phillips didn't even ask this time, but just handed Calabar a third cartridge, seemingly unable to tear his eyes away from the torn-up oak tree. Moments later, a third ball found its mark, just between the first two, and Phillips clapped Calabar on the shoulder.

"I don't know how you came by it, friend, but you have a positive gift for shooting. I think that I was right and we need to find you a proper rifle, to see whether your aim is as good as your luck." He took the Bess back from Calabar and sighted down the barrel at the tree again himself.

"I couldn't make those shots, and I've been using this very gun for three years. I've always thought that this weapon's just no good for that kind of work."

Calabar shrugged in reply. Although he controlled the grin that wanted to burst across his face, for fear of appearing to be too proud, his heart was fairly bursting. Here was something that he could actually do well, besides making indigo.

While he was learning it with the intent of using it for the pursuit of war against the Crown and all that it represented, he knew that these skills would be useful in providing for his family as well, and it gave him deep comfort to know that he would be able to take care of them, even if the indigo trade should falter, or Cooper decide that he no longer needed their partnership.

Too, Calabar knew that it meant that he would never have to hide in his own home, should it be discovered by either the King's men or what Indians still lived in these parts. If he could but secure a Bess for himself, he could truly see to their safety, and that knowledge made him feel truly free for the first time since he had gotten the papers that recorded Greene's manumission of him.

Chapter 23

Most of the other men of the Committee of Safety accepted Calabar with little comment. Even the most standoffish of them had become downright friendly when Phillips had described his skill with a gun, and once the Committee found him a rifle to use, it only took a couple of demonstrations of his skill before he was widely celebrated as the man to go to if a distant target needed special attention.

Affey was less than thrilled at his new-found occupation, however. "How can it help me, how can you keep Fantee safe, if you are struck down by some chance bullet? I don't doubt that things will come to open warfare, now that the King's militia is rampaging through the countryside, but must you be the one to answer it?"

It took him a moment to come up with an answer that he could put into words, but looking at her face, where he could still see the fading bruises, he knew that he would not again stand idly by while she was beaten senseless, nor would he willingly find himself in the position of being unable to protect himself. The loss of their baby was an unspoken, deeper pain – they had not discussed it since he had brought her back to the cabin.

"I must do this, Affey. Others have done more than I can and I can do more than some we know. I will not hide in our home and hope that somebody else cares for your safety and Fantee's as

I do."

Affey did not reply, but continued sewing a patch onto the knee of Calabar's trousers that had been split when they had been attacked, her mouth a grim, tight line. He saw her steely glare rove over to the rifle where it stood beside the door, its cartridge case hanging on a peg beside it.

He sighed inwardly. Was there any way to explain to her just how helpless and lost he had felt at her bedside, wondering whether all that he had sacrificed to bring her out of peril was for naught? Could she understand the impulse – no, the obligation – he felt to put himself between her and any possible harm?

Fantee came toddling across the room toward them and tripped on her own feet, falling and letting out a shriek. Affey was at her side almost before she hit the ground, comforting her and standing her back on her feet. Calabar saw in a moment of utter clarity that she did understand, probably more completely than he did. He also saw that she knew what was at stake if he were to fail her in the process.

He felt a burst of empathy toward her, and as she stood up from taking care of the child, he strode over and pulled her into his arms. She was stiff with her anger at him at first, her arms at her sides and barely even acknowledging his embrace. He murmured, "I need to do this, Affey, just as you need to be Fantee's protector. It is my responsibility – and my privilege – to stand between you both and the dangers of a world that is going mad before our very eyes."

She softened in his arms then, and as her own arms rose to return his embrace, he could feel her body quaking with sobs. He held her, stroking her head and her shoulder for comfort. Finally, as her weeping subsided, she choked out the question, "Why did we come to live in such wicked times, in the middle of a struggle that is not of our making?"

Calabar considered his answer carefully, and then spoke slowly and clearly, as much for himself as for Affey. "We are fortunate, I think, to see such times. By being a part of the events of these days, we can change them, help to ensure that Fantee, and her children and grandchildren, are not obliged to endure such hardships in their turn."

Affey pulled back enough to look him in the eye, disbelief in her expression. "Do you really think that we can make this world a better place for her? Do you believe that if we do, it will stay a better place for her children and their heirs? What I have seen of this world is that it is wickedness, relieved only a little by the occasional spot of good."

Calabar examined her face, again thinking carefully about his words, ensuring that he knew his own mind before he spoke. "I do not disagree that we have tasted much of wickedness in the world around us. However, we have had more than our share of kindness and good as well. It may be that in the end, the balance tips toward evil over good, but that will never change if we do not act to change it."

He sought out her eyes with his gaze, speaking with emphasis. "This is why I must join the fight."

She took a deep breath and nodded reluctantly, and he pulled her back into his arms.

Chapter 24

Calabar tried to keep his mind on the work before him and not concern himself with the events that lay outside his control, but after the end of a drill, he could not help but ask Cooper, "Have you been heard anything new about those men who hurt my Anna?"

Cooper shook his head. "Most of those rowdies have slunk back to their farms and know better than to show their faces in town, now that Governor Martin has made to run to go hide in the fort up at the mouth of the river."

He spat for emphasis, adding, "A few of them have followed the governor up to that area, no doubt hoping to curry favor by offering their support, but the Committee of Safety is running things along the rest of the river now."

Calabar nodded. "I be glad to hear that they not be making any more trouble for Anna or me."

Cooper shrugged. "None of us is safe until this matter is concluded and the King and his brutes here stop trying to deny us the freedom we've seized." He looked Calabar steadily in the eye. "Before this is over, we will likely have to face the King's men in earnest, and not just play at drill here. Are you ready for that day?"

Calabar returned the other man's gaze. "I be ready keep Anna and my baby safe. If that mean that I got shoot some man,

I shoot."

Cooper looked away, his lips pursed. "We may hope that it doesn't come to that, but I am glad that your wife and baby have you to defend them." He motioned at the rifle slung over Calabar's back. "You are all fortunate that you have proven to have the gift of making the most of that."

Calabar didn't say anything, but he was far from certain that it was a gift to be skilled at the use of an instrument of death.

"I best be gone home," he said. "Anna be nervous when I go out."

Cooper waved his hand to the road. "Please, don't let me hold you. By all means, you must attend to the comfort and happiness of your wife."

"Thank you, Mister Cooper," Calabar said, turning to leave.

"Until next time, Jupiter. You're a good man, and I'm glad to have you on our side in this." Cooper raised his hand in a gesture of respect, and Calabar pondered as he started home on the strange fact that he had gone from a piece of property reckoned as being worth a handful of coins to a valued friend, from little more than a brute laborer to a skilled freeholder.

After he turned off the road and onto the track that led to his home, he felt himself begin to relax somewhat, although he remained vigilant enough. So, when he saw a flicker of movement out of the corner of his eye, he froze, his hands reaching reflexively for the rifle.

Straining his eyes in the direction of the movement, he saw a deer, its ears flicking nervously as it tried to decide whether or not Calabar was a threat. Apparently satisfied, it returned to reaching up for the fresh shoots of growth on a tree. Calabar could see that its antlers were just starting to grow out for the year, and was glad that the creature was far from his carefully prepared garden plot.

Although deer were not inclined to eat indigo, they were eager devourers of food crops, and Calabar could remember one year when a rampaging herd had wiped out nearly all of the vegetables that the slaves on the plantation had planted to supplement their meager rations.

This one looked to be perhaps in its third year, large enough to reach the lower branches of the tree it was eating from, and Calabar found himself slowly lifting the rifle down to load it. This one animal would feed his family through most of the summer, and the rich addition to their diet would help Affey to finish healing.

He told himself that he was far enough from town that he need not worry about drawing unwelcome attention with a shot, and the deer appeared to have dismissed him as any sort of threat at all, so focused was it on the tender leaves and branches it was eating. While the powder and shot he carried were meant to be used only for drill – or in case of actual combat – Phillips had told him that he could replace both in trade, if some need arose for him to use them for his own purposes.

Calabar eased the lock back slowly, suppressing the click of its mechanism with his hand wrapped around the stock. He lifted the rifle to his shoulder, took aim, and slowly pulled the trigger.

When the smoke cleared, Calabar was gratified to see that the deer had dropped, with no more movement than a death twitch, and was not struggling or fleeing. He nodded in satisfaction and swung the rifle back over his shoulder, once he had cleaned the pan and touch-hole, just as Phillips had showed him.

That chore attended to, he waited for a long moment to listen carefully to ensure that nothing – and nobody – had been drawn by the sound of gunfire. Despite his self-reassurance, it was unusual enough a sound outside of town that he wanted to be cautious against the possibility that some unfriendly ear might have been nearby enough to have heard it. The creatures of the woods were returning to their normal scurrying and singing, though, filling the silence that had followed the blast of his rifle. Calaban nodded to himself in satisfaction and moved toward the spot where the deer had fallen.

He crouched next to the carcass, considering whether to try to remove the offal before lifting it. The animal was not a large one – the velvet-covered antlers growing from its head each had a spread just bigger than his outstretched hand – and he grunted as he pulled the carcass over onto its back and looked at it.

He'd never dressed anything as big as a deer before, but he imagined that the principles were the same, just on a larger scale. He wished that Affey were with him, though, as she had a lot more experience than he did with such matters. It didn't seem that heavy as he moved it around, though, and he tried hefting it.

The animal draped over his shoulder easily enough, and he decided to bring it home intact, so that he could rely on Affey's greater knowledge of the ways of food preparation. He told himself that it had nothing to do with his squeamishness at the thought of having to pull the creature's guts out and separate the edible from the scrap.

Quickly enough, he had emerged into the clearing where their home stood, and found Affey standing anxiously at the door, their daughter peering out past her apron. At the sight of Calaban with his prize on his back, the anxiety on Affey's face transformed to joy.

She ran to him, crying out, "You shot that?"

Calabar bent to deposit the carcass before her. He stood, hearing the pride in own his voice as he answered, "I did, yes – we should eat well for a while now."

She frowned and murmured, "When I heard the shot, I thought that something bad had happened. Again." He stepped around the deer and gathered her into his arms.

"No, Affey, nothing bad happened, and with me being under arms and part of the Committee's militia, we are safer now than we have ever been." Fantee had followed her mother out of the house and was now curiously stroking the deer's fur.

Affey pulled away from Calabar to scold her. "You leave that poor thing alone, Fantee. Your papa and I need to turn it into food, so you go on back inside now."

Fantee stood up and looked up at Calabar. "Soft, papa," she said, drawing a grin from Calabar.

"Yes, Fantee, deer have soft fur, but the rabbit has softer. Go on inside like your mama said."

The baby toddled back inside, and Affey pushed her sleeves back, nodding over to Calabar. "Best get out of your good clothes, and get that shirt soaking to stop the stain from setting." Calabar looked down, and was chagrined to see that the buck had bled onto his shirt.

While he changed and put the shirt in a bucket with some clean water, Affey was sharpening her knife, and when they were both ready, he followed her out to where the deer waited. He watched in fascination and pride as she squared up the carcass and got to work, occasionally giving him quiet commands to help her hold or cut.

Within a matter of minutes, she was tossing scraps to the chickens and cutting the meat into long strips. "I'll dry that, so that it keeps for later in the year," she remarked over her shoulder. The edible organs she set aside on her clean second apron, along with a good-sized haunch from one of the legs.

She gathered it up and stood. "Stay here with the rest, to be sure that it doesn't draw scavengers. I'll get these started and then finish up what's left." Calabar nodded as she left. The carcass was a lot less disturbing now that it just looked like meat. The skin was splayed out – he wished idly that he had the knowledge of how to cure it for leather – and the chickens were worrying at the head where Affey had tossed it to them.

She returned and stooped back down to start cutting through a joint, saying, "We'll eat well tonight, and I want to get this cut into pieces that we can bring in for the night. Can't do anything with the skin before it goes off. Back home –" she caught herself, and then continued "– back at Mister Greene's plantation, I would have saved it for old Okree, but since we don't have him around here, I'll let it go to waste."

She sighed and turned back to look up at Calabar. "I'm sorry, Calabar, I didn't mean to say Mister Greene's house was 'home.'"

Calabar shook his head dismissively. "It was our home for longer than this has been, and I know that you miss the company of the others back on the plantation." He stretched. "I miss some of them, too, although I hope not to see them all too soon."

Affey stopped what she was doing and gave him a questioning

look. Calabar said quietly, "Governor's offering a reward to any slave who takes up arms in his service, I heard in town. Might even be willing to buy their freedom for them, someone said."

He shrugged. "Might all just be idle talk, and it's hard to know whether Master Greene would even let word of such a thing be read to the boys back at the plantation, but I'm just saying that I'd rather not encounter any of them from the wrong end of a musket."

Affey frowned deeply, her expression betraying grave concern. "I'm not worried on your account, Calabar, but could you really bring yourself to shoot down Shampee or one of the boys, should they be at the wrong end of your gun?"

Calabar nodded in agreement. "Exactly. Which I why I said that I hope not to see any of them any time soon." He sighed. "The whole world is in an uproar, and it's hard enough without worrying about things that may be nothing more than rumor, though. For now, let's finish up with this deer, and enjoy the fruits of our good fortune."

Affey's mouth pursed as though she were considering a retort, but she bent back to the work at hand. Calabar knew that he hadn't heard the last of the matter and wished that he'd kept the rumor to himself.

Chapter 25

A trickle of sweat made its way down Calabar's forehead as he walked in loose formation in the morning heat with the rest of the company. As narrow as the road was here, they were stretched out into a long line of militia troops, each man bearing a variety of rucksacks and each with a gun over his shoulder.

The summer heat was oppressive, but there was a certain lightness to his step as Calabar walked. They were off to strike a blow directly against Governor Martin and his intolerable plan to arm slaves, in order to keep the entire colony in servitude to the Crown.

Word had reached town of open warfare having erupted in Massachusetts-Bay Colony, far away to the north. It was said that a British force had fired on and slaughtered a militia gathering, but that the men of the district all about had struck back as the British returned to Boston, wiping out the majority of the red-coated marauders. Calabar didn't know how much of the accounts he heard could be believed, but one thing was clear – the conflict was no longer a mere matter of local rabble chasing out a governor, but was a war against the full might and fury of the Crown.

In response, Governor Martin had taken refuge at Fort Johnston. Seeing an opportunity, a Colonel Ashe in the neighboring town was mounting an expedition against the governor's forces at

Fort Johnston, and he made it known that he was looking for men. As soon as Calabar had heard about it, he'd told Affey, and had explained that this was a chance to prevent the specter of facing a friend across the battle lines. She had reluctantly granted him leave to join up, but had stayed inside with Fantee when he'd left, refusing to make a big affair of his departure.

The force in which Calabar was marching was some five hundred strong, and his heart swelled to see so many joined in the effort to capture the governor and, in the process, strike a blow against the Crown that enabled him to oppress the people of North-Carolina. Of course, there were different degrees of freedom that the men of the expedition were fighting for.

Calabar had noticed some of the militiamen giving him open looks of suspicion, and had even heard one man mutter to his fellow, "Who thought it a good idea to give a negro a gun – isn't that what we march against the governor over?"

Cooper, though, had overheard, and had whirled on the militiaman. "Can you strike down a squirrel at a hundred paces? Mister Jupiter here can, which makes it a capital idea to have armed him with a rifle and to have included him in our company. Have you any other questions?" He glared fiercely at the man, who held up his hands in a mollifying gesture.

"I meant nothing by it, sir," the man said, ducking his head in obeisance. "Can he really hit a squirrel at a hundred paces?"

Cooper shrugged. "Ask him yourself." He turned away dismissively.

Calabar narrowed his eyes as though pondering the question, and then said, "There be not much left of a squirrel, should I be shoot one with this." He patted the butt of the rifle, adding, "I been hit the heart of a deer about that far from me last month, though."

After the militiaman nodded in acknowledgement, Calabar reached into his rucksack and pulled out a strip of venison jerky, grinning. "It be still taste good." The other man answered with a hoarse bark of laughter.

"I don't doubt it does," he said, slapping Calabar on the back. "But mind you, a trained soldier firing back at you from the safety of a fort is a far more chancy target than a buck standing in the woods."

Calabar nodded, his expression suddenly grave. "I been knowed that." He swallowed hard and added, "I be hoping my aim is still steady, when it be a man I want to shoot."

"I suppose that we shall all be dependent upon your steady aim, by and by." The man gestured toward the head of the column. "If Colonel Ashe's plans come to fruition, we shall soon enough be serving those fellows who have stood by the governor hot and hot, and your rifle balls will be among the hottest fire we can offer them."

Cooper turned back around. "Let's have no idle talk about the colonel's plans, now. Surprise is our best friend in this action, and the very trees have ears. You go on up to the next unit and make sure that everyone gets the word that we should have no open discussion of what the colonel intends to do."

"Yes, sir," said the man, and broke into an easy jog, his expression inscrutable.

Cooper said in an undertone, "Jupiter, never you mind what these loudmouths say. Your gun will be put to a proper use at the proper time, and when the time comes for you to employ it, you'll have no lack of company."

Calabar nodded. "I be not worrying about suchlike," he said. "I be trust you, trust colonel. Governor and his rowdies be have to worrying." He smiled and Cooper returned the smile.

"Just so, Jupiter, just so." Both men fell silent, focusing again on the rhythmic tread of shoes on the road, a pattern of sound that seemed to reduce the effort of walking mile after mile toward their destination.

By the time that the sun was starting to lower in the late afternoon sky, the company was marching alongside the river, and they came around a bend in the road that revealed their target, the fort where Governor Martin and his forces had taken refuge. A British ship stood at anchor behind it in the river, its sails furled and its colors hanging limply from the rearmost mast.

Colonel Ashe sent out word for the company to assemble as a force before him, and climbed up onto a wagon to be seen and heard by all. His voice carried easily to the back ranks of the assembled company, and filled them with the confidence he exuded.

"Gentlemen, there before you is the stronghold of our oppression in North-Carolina. Governor Martin believes that he can hold us in terror and submission from within its walls, but I mean to reduce those walls, before this day is out, to little more than a pile of ash."

He smiled slightly at the laughter that erupted at his play on his own name, and then continued. "There are good guns within, and I should like to preserve them – cannon will become the currency of our liberation – but I would not like to trade even one of you men for all of those guns."

He held his hands out in a gesture of mock resignation. "If the governor chooses to leave them behind in his haste to evade us, so much the better. If we drive him from Carolina soil but lose the guns, we will have won the day. And if we only fire the walls, and both the man and his guns elude us, I shall be satisfied."

He looked over his shoulder at the fort. "Right now, the governor is likely trying to make out what we here are about. I propose that we should answer that question without delay. Form up by unit, and prepare your muskets. At my signal, we shall give them a salute, and then the opportunity to withdraw like civilized men. Aim for the walls, that your fire may be heard, but we do not yet shoot to kill."

He grinned savagely. "If they do not take our offer, we shall draw near enough to make it smart and repeat it; after that, I imagine that the action will determine its own path naturally enough. Very well, enough chatter, form up."

He stepped down from the wagon and mounted his horse. After the men of the company had each found their place and stood silent and eager, he cried out, "Make ready!" As one, the men swung their guns down from their shoulders and went through the mechanical motions of loading live rounds into their guns.

Calabar could see that more than one man around him attended to his gun with shaking hands, and he was unsurprised to find that his own hands shook slightly as he completed the practiced steps with his rifle. He was a touch slower than some of the men behind him, but he was not the last to shoulder his weapon, ready for the command, "Aim!"

Calabar picked the British flag at the top of the staff above the fort as his target. While he did not expect to hit it at this range he figured that the men within would take more dismay from harm to the flag than they would just another ball striking the walls of the fort.

"And fire!" The colonel's voice was drowned out by the roar of nearly simultaneous fire from hundreds of guns. As the balls struck, raising a line of dust and debris, Calabar was unsurprised to see that nearly all of them had fallen far short of the fort itself. However, he knew that anyone inside the fort would have to be thinking that another round from a closer range would be far more deadly in effect.

After the smoke from the volley had cleared somewhat, he saw the flag flutter down from the staff and nearly cried out aloud – had his shot indeed found its target? The men all around him shouted out in one voice at the sight, and Calabar saw the colonel wheel his horse around, his mouth set in an expression of grim satisfaction.

The man nearest to Calabar must have seen the confusion on his face, for he explained, "They've cut down their flag," he said, excited. "The fort is ours."

The colonel echoed his words a moment later. "The governor is a wiser man than I knew," he said. "The fort is ours; we will give them a decent interval to make good their departure, and then we shall go and seize what they have left behind."

A small column of figures emerged from the gates of the fort and boarded launches from the ship. Calabar thought with a shock of recognition that one of them might have been Master Greene, but at the distance from which he watched, he could not be certain.

As soon as the launches pushed off from the shore, the colonel dismounted and pointed at a number of men in turn, seemingly favoring the strongest-looking he could spot. "You men, come with me, and we shall see whether anything of value remains . . . and ensure that nothing of value is left when we depart."

The militiamen with the colonel moved eagerly across the distance between the body of the expedition and the quiet fort. They entered through the open gate, and after just a few minutes, Calabar noted columns of smoke rising from every corner of the structure.

The militia emerged and moved systematically around the walls, torches in hand, firing the fort at every point where they could reach something flammable. Two men broke away from the fort to set a small house outside its walls ablaze, and then rejoined the detachment to march back.

They returned to the company, faces shining with glee, behind the colonel, who again mounted the wagon. "Governor Martin left nothing of value behind, and obviously had some intelligence of our intentions this day. In any event, he has removed all of the guns and stores to his ship out there, and my next object is to effect the removal of that ship back to England, where it belongs!"

The men huzzahed and then fell silent as Colonel Ashe raised a hand for quiet. "I should have liked to assemble fire rafts to launch toward the ship and encourage its master to depart, but without a breeze to move them, there is little point in pursuing that plan. We could offer another volley of musketry, but the possibility that they might answer with grapeshot from the ship's cannon is too great, and their range is greater than ours."

He sighed. "We shall have to wait for another opportunity to drive out the governor entirely, but for today, let us celebrate that his feet no longer curse the sacred soil of Carolina and that we are, as of this moment, free of the yoke of British tyranny!"

Around Calabar, the men of the detachment broke out into another round of huzzahs, and solemn handshakes gave way swiftly to joyful embraces and back-pounding hugs. Even the man who had questioned Calabar's use of a firearm sought him out and offered him a hug, a conciliatory smile on his face. Calabar returned the embrace, overcome at the sensation of having taken part in such a momentous event.

Chapter 26

The autumn rains had been good to Calabar's garden, though he could not say the same for his shoes. Affey quietly hissed her disapproval and frustration as she carefully scraped away the mud of another slog into town for drill with the militia. The fire crackled merrily in their hearth, though, and Fantee was playing quietly with her doll, instructing it in the niceties of eating at the adult table.

Calabar was mending the knee of yet another pair of breeches, this time sewing on a neat patch to cover the hole he'd ripped when he'd tripped on a loose rock while practicing loading while advancing, under Cooper's watchful eye. While he could never hope to match the speed of the musket troops, he was getting better and better.

He tied off the thread and trimmed it with his teeth, and then held up the breeches to examine his handiwork. He nodded to himself, satisfied, and folded them neatly to drape over the back of a chair.

Colonel Ashe had seen to the equipping of the regiment – it was said that he'd done so without asking the Committee of Safety for any repayment – and so the quartermaster had procured and distributed serviceable, solid breeches, shirts, shoes, and even a proper coat for each of the members of the regiment.

Calabar felt a particular sense of frustration with himself

therefore, at having split the knee of the new breeches, and so he had given the repair extra care. Bad enough that some of the militiamen in the regiment clearly considered themselves his betters; there was no need for him to look the part.

Although some of the members of the regiment had gotten new weapons as part of the colonel's equipping, the rifle Calabar had been given to use was judged to be adequate. He was just as glad, as he'd gotten used to its particular foibles, and did not relish trying to break in a new weapon. As he glanced over at where it stood beside the door, he wondered idly whether he'd be able to keep it when the war with England was over.

He supposed that if the rebellion failed, he might well join his fellow militiamen on a gallows, but he gave that thought no serious consideration, so confident he felt under the leadership of Colonel Ashe and alongside his friend Cooper.

His friend had set aside his mercantile business in favor of full-time service in the militia. Privately, he told Calabar that he had savings set aside sufficient to permit him the luxury, but Calabar somehow suspected that Cooper would have gladly descended into poverty once he committed himself fully to the cause of independence.

Cooper's fervor had taken Calabar by surprise at first, but on reflection, he supposed that it was sensible enough. The Crown's capricious barriers to commerce and movement were not generally good for trade, despite their relatively good fortune at leveraging the blockades in New-England to their own advantage.

Thinking on the question further, Calabar wondered if his friend might not even have been moved to action by seeing the misfortune of warfare visited on himself and Affey . . . and their lost baby. He sat with the realization of that possibility for a long time, so long that he found Affey looking at him curiously.

"What has your mind so powerfully engaged that you did not even hear me call your name the first time, Calabar?"

He smiled ruefully and answered, "I'm sorry. I was just thinking about how even the misfortunes of people like us can change the lives of people who are . . . not like us."

She snorted. "You mean like Master Greene?"

"No." He shook his head. "We haven't changed Master Greene's life one bit that I can see. I was thinking of Mister Cooper and even Mister Allbright. They were good men before they met us, I think, but I wonder whether they became even better when they saw that there was a need for them to do so?"

Affey shook her head. "I don't see how it makes any difference, one way or another. The King's men would have burned out Mister Allbright whether or not you ever came to town, and Mister Cooper would have joined up with the Committee just because he didn't like to see the likes of Master Greene get away with murder."

Calabar sighed, still feeling a stab of anguish at the mention of Allbright's vicious fate. "I suppose you are right, though I'd surely like to think that my influence extends a little ways past the clearing around this house."

She smiled gently. "Your influence doesn't need to spread over all the world for it to be enough for me, Calabar. I wish you could be happy with what you have here, and leave questions of influence to folks who have the luxury of dabbling in such matters."

"I am happy with what I have here, and I am doing this only because I don't ever want to lose it." He tried to keep the edge of irritation he felt at the renewal of her old complaint out of his voice, but could hear that he was failing to do so. He took a deep breath and closed his eyes, his mouth pursed, as he struggled to find the words to explain the matter to her.

He held up his hands in a mollifying gesture. "My happiness does not depend upon how much influence I have, but from knowing that I am looking to your safety myself, and not depending on others to care about you as much as I do. Do you see that?"

It was Affey's turn to consider her words carefully for a moment. "I just don't like seeing you leave us here to go and expose yourself to risks that I would rather we face together. I do understand that you want to take this burden onto your own shoulders alone, but I am willing to share it with you."

He sighed again. "I have a gift, Affey, one that few of the men of the regiment share, and one that is put to its best use within the ranks of the militia, not just here at our own door." She frowned at him, and he wondered at the fact that he'd never shared with her his unique ability with a gun.

He pointed at the rifle. "Have you noticed that the gun I carry is different from the ones that most everyone has?"

She shook her head. "I've not seen the other men with their guns. And if I had, I would have guessed that it was because they wanted your gun to be less effective than theirs, since you are only a freedman."

He chuckled. "No, Affey. Mine is far more effective than most of theirs. And do you know why they gave me this better gun?"

"No, I do not."

He smiled grimly. "Because I can hit targets that other men cannot." He told her about the day when he'd first fired a gun, how he'd hit the same tree three times running. Her eyebrows went up when he explained that Phillips, the gunsmith, had said that he couldn't have hit it even once.

"So you see, this is why I say that I have an obligation to take part in this fight. It is not a question of influence, but one of duty. Duty to the friend who has died already, and duty to the friends who have put their lives at hazard to see to the freedom of not just themselves, but us as well."

Affey's head dropped and she closed her eyes in resignation. Opening them, she looked back up at him. "Yes, Calabar, I see. I'll not question it again, no matter how much it pains me to close the door after you leave for drill or for the next expedition. Just . . . come back to me, please."

He stood and pulled her up into an embrace. "Of course, my dearest friend. That is my greatest duty of all."

He held her, his eyes closed, for what seemed like an eternity. He had no greater duty, indeed.

Chapter 27

The first deep purple light of the dawn was just showing through the trees when the sound of a musket blast split the air like a thunderclap. Calabar awoke with a start, his heart pounding in his chest as he leapt to his feet. His hands found his gun, his fingers questing briefly over the mechanism to verify that all was ready to load a shot.

Like everyone around him, he peered into the fog toward the creek, straining to see where the blast had originated. He could not even tell if it was from the gun of a friend or foe. That question was answered as the call was passed along the line in urgent whispers.

"The Scots are coming! Make ready!"

Indeed, through the dark and fog, Calabar could now hear an eerie wailing, a sound unlike any he had heard before, and he realized that this must be the "pipes" that some of the men of the regiment had told him to expect with their approach. He listened with half an ear as he went through the mechanical, rote steps of loading his rifle, glad for the long hours of practice that had made doing it without any useful light relatively easy.

He'd seen a variety of whistles and flutes that the slaves on Master Greene's plantation had fashioned for themselves, but he could not picture how any of these could make the hair-raising sounds that now filtered through the woods. "Looks and sounds like a man has a cat tucked under his arm, and is making sport of the poor beast," one old militiaman had told him, which made more sense than anything else Calabar could imagine, based on what he now heard.

The light improved slightly as the sounds of the approaching Loyalist forces grew louder, and Calabar almost imagined he could see the bridge. The company had already taken steps to discourage any organized force from making effective use of the passage over the creek, though, pulling up the planks and greasing the underlying timbers. Calabar had thought this a silly exercise the day before, but had kept his counsel.

He got his first glimpse of the enemy as they approached the far side of the bridge, and heard the whispered command, "Hold your fire, men." The column came to a stop at the bridge, the sound of the pipes swirling to finish, and it was clear that what had seemed to Calabar like little more than a mischievous prank at the time had now interrupted the progress of the Loyalist forces.

In a matter of a few minutes, though, the man to Calabar's left whispered, "Here they come," and indeed, he could just see the Loyalists charging toward the bridge in a tight formation, swords held high. Through the mist, he could hear their battle cry.

"Broadswords and King George!" Their brogues rendered the words hard to make out, but even as he puzzled through what they were yelling, he had to wonder at their foolishness. Did they not know that they faced muskets and even artillery at the far side of the bridge?

"Hold . . . hold . . . "

The first of the Loyalists tried the denuded timbers of the bridge, and Calabar could hear shouts and curses of surprise followed by splashes and cries for help as some of them discovered the slippery trap laid for them there. The charge broke, but those remaining on the bank now split between those who tried wading into the creek and those who more cautiously picked their way across the narrow, slippery timbers.

Still, the whispers went up and down the line, "Hold . . . hold . . . " Calabar was sighting down his rifle at his chosen target, a man whose sash and brightwork seemed to set him apart from the others.

It wasn't until that man had taken up a position at the head of the reformed column, again raising his blade high and crying out more clearly now, "Broadswords and King George!" that the blast of the patriot cannon rent the morning air again, the flash of its muzzle briefly illuminating the column behind him, even as it struck many of them down in an instant.

Calabar's finger tightened on his trigger, and his shot rang out along with those of dozens, even hundreds of others in a staccato echo of the cannon's roar. He saw his target fall like a child's discarded doll, and turned away to attend to the task of reloading his gun.

As his hands worked, he saw his man fall again in his mind's eye, and he found that he was shaking when he again shouldered his gun. He had taken a man's life. The man he had shot would never again feel the caress of a lover's hand, nor feel the soft breeze of a quiet evening. Instead of returning to feast and laugh in whatever home he had lived in, the man would molder in a cold grave in this unremarkable copse of trees.

Nothing Calabar could do would un-fire that shot; nothing could restore things to the way that they had been a minute before. Even as these thoughts crowded through his mind, though, he forced himself to focus on the job at hand. The remaining Loyalists were recovering themselves and charging forward, and more men were appearing on the far side of the creek, some of them already aiming muskets toward the Patriot forces.

He picked another target and steadied himself, trying to ignore the rippling crack of gunfire from both sides of the creek. A Loyalist ball whistled past him and he took a deep breath, willing himself to calm as his finger applied pressure again to the fatal trigger.

The light was better now, and the fog of the morning was being supplanted by the smoke of hundreds of muskets. Men were yelling around him – and screaming from the other side as they lay dying or wounded. His rifle shot almost came as a surprise to him, and another man fell.

Calabar felt no pride at his marksmanship now that it had found its true purpose. He only felt numbness in the place where his heart ought to have been hammering, and when his rifle again rose to his shoulder, loaded, primed, and ready, he had no memory of having prepared it.

He sighted down the barrel again, and found himself looking through the morning light and battle smoke at a familiar face, and it seemed to him as though time itself stopped.

Master Greene stood on the far shore, his arm raised to urge someone to join the retreat, and Calabar studied the man's face in wonder and shock. He'd known that Greene was part of the Loyalist militia that had answered Governor Martin's call for service. He'd thought that he had seen the man at the retreat from Fort Johnston, and it struck him as somehow fitting that he should see him again fleeing from a fight.

He remembered Greene's face when the man had had his own gun sighted on Calabar's chest, and he remembered with cold anger the violence Greene and his companions had visited upon poor Simbee, and later, Affey and himself. He felt the cool metal of the trigger under his fingertip, and the polished grain of the stock against his cheek. He could smell powder and his own fearful sweat, and he was aware of the almost lazy "lub-dub" of his heart as time started up again.

He released his breath and shifted his gun to aim at the man beside Greene. That man fell, screaming his anguish at a ruined leg that blossomed scarlet through his white breeches. Calabar saw Greene's head turn toward him, and saw the man's eyes widen in recognition as he saw his former slave, saw the rifle in his hands, and saw the choice that Calabar had made.

Satisfied, Calabar lowered his gun, and was unsurprised as the call came down the line, "Cease fire! We have won the day! Cease fire!" He set the rifle down carefully on the ground and stood silently, looking at Greene, as the men around him erupted in huzzahs and other shouts of celebration.

Greene broke eye contact with him, and again turned to urge the men around him to retreat. Calabar saw the survivors on the Patriot-controlled side of the bridge being rounded up, and watched a team hurry to the bridge with the planking carried between them. He felt almost disinterested as they began throwing the planks back onto the bridge so that the Patriot forces could pursue their vanquished foes.

One of the men beside him slapped him on the back, laughter in his eyes, and said, "Ain't you going to come along and make sure that them boys don't all get away to fight again tomorrow? Come on!"

Calabar nodded dumbly and bent to sling his rifle over his shoulder, but he felt no joy in the death and ruin in which he had partaken. Nor did he feel any particular satisfaction at having spared Greene. In fact, he wondered, as he joined the Patriot column thudding across the loose planks of the restored bridge after the Loyalist forces, when he would feel anything at all again.

Chapter 28

The spring sunshine warmed Calabar's back as he moved along the tidy rows of his garden. The vulnerable shoots of his sprouting mustard greens had attracted multitudes of small yellow and black beetles, and he feared that they would decimate his crop before it even had time to get fairly started.

Shuffling along on his knees beside the row of plants, he carefully picked each beetle off and flicked it away toward the woods. There was a time when he would have squashed them between his finger and thumb, or dropped them into a bucket of water to drown, but that was before.

Fantee chased a chicken past the garden, shrieking with delight as the nimble bird outran her, clucking in alarm and beating its wings to aid its escape. Calabar sat back on his heels and watched her, a gentle smile coming over his face. Past her, he could see Affey at the door, looking out with concern etched on her face, to see what the fuss was about.

He had promised to keep them safe, and he nodded to himself in satisfaction. He'd kept that promise, and the war had returned to a comfortable distance, disrupting his friend Cooper's trade mightily, but having little ongoing impact on Calabar's quiet homestead at the outskirts of their community.

Calabar had returned the rifle to Philips and had withdrawn from the militia, deaf to the praises heaped on him. He knew that he had done all that he could in the service of the rebellion against a distant king, and unless that fight returned to his doorstep, he could see no further part in it for himself.

Affey caught his eye from where she stood in the doorway of their home and smiled. Calabar smiled in reply. This was all the meaning that freedom needed to hold for him.

Also in Audiobook

Many readers love the experience of turning the pages in a paper book such as the one you hold in your hands. Others enjoy hearing a skilled narrator tell them a story, bringing the words on the page to life.

Brief Candle Press has arranged to have *The Freedman* produced as a high-quality audiobook, and you can listen to a sample and learn where to purchase it in that form by scanning the QR code below with your phone, tablet, or other device, or going to the Web address shown.

Happy listening!

bit.ly/TheFreedmanAudio

Historical Notes

North-Carolina saw little in the way of major action during the American Revolution, but the men and women of the colony were no less energetic than their neighbors in supporting the cause of independence and freedom.

They certainly had a stronger claim than some of their neighbors to having deep roots in an opposition movement to the colonial government, and the old Regulators were still pretty stirred up over Governor Martin's self-serving extravagance when the unrest in the New-England colonies started to boil over into open rebellion.

It is a cruel irony that even as North-Carolinians supported the cause of liberty, their colonial government denied its blessings to those enslaved and those who had exited that servitude alike. North-Carolina's laws were among the harshest in the colonies in restricting its freedmen, and the legal protections afforded to slaves were almost entirely focused on ensuring that slaveholders were compensated for harm that might befall the men and women owned.

There were some who objected on philosophical grounds to the institution of slavery, but they were not nearly as outspoken in North-Carolina as they were in the New-England colonies. Both the rebels and the Crown forces accepted black recruits, and the governor even went so far as to offer freedom to slaves who fought against the rebellion, but few were offered arms or a place in the lines.

There were, as mentioned in passing, settlements of freedmen and runaways in the swamps, but for many of those who escaped slavery one way or the other, the only viable path was to leave North-Carolina as soon as humanly possible. It's possible that a few lived, as Calabar and Affey did, in homesteads secreted away in the forests outside of more-heavily settled areas, but I cannot point to any specific evidence of this.

Acknowledgements

Writing about the travails of African-Americans in a colony dependent on slavery from an era nearly two and a half centuries past involves trying to put myself into the place of people whose experiences have little in common with my own. What is in common, however, is our humanity, our capacity for decency in the face of emnity, and our hope for a better world for our children.

Trying to build on what my limited experience has provided me to understand the experience of my characters required me to take a deep dive into the legal and cultural framework in which they operated. I am deeply grateful for the detailed, unflinching and very unpleasant record of the treatment of slaves and freedmen that is included in *Slavery in North Carolina 1748-1775*, compiled by Marvin L. Michael Kay and Lorin Lee Cary.

Helping to bolster my understanding what could have driven people so mistreated to stand up and join in the fight for independence were the many accounts of such individuals gathered by Bobby G. Moss and Michael C. Scoggins in their book *African-American Patriots in the Southern Campaign of the American Revolution.*

I started writing *The Freedman* outside of my normal cycle after a fellow author of the Colonial South, Sara Whitford, posted a news account that caught my imagination and wouldn't let it go. The former mayor of Greenville, Ed Carter, learned that his free black ancestor had fought on the Patriot side in the American Revolution, and this knowledge has inspired him to found the first African-American chapter of the Sons of the American Revolution.

His story of finding inspiration in this discovery immediately compelled me to sit down and start sketching out *The Freedman.* From this exercise, I have learned that I am terrible at writing outlines, but that a great story will enable me to complete a challenging work regardless of my prior plans.

Sincere thanks to my co-star in the Discovery Network's miniseries *The American Revolution,* Jeff Clarke, who drew on his knowledge of Revolution-era firearms to review the passage regarding the loading sequence for the Brown Bess.

Sara Whitford, in addition to having given me the genesis of this work, was incredibly generous with her time and expertise in the time and place where it was set. It has been a genuine joy to discuss both with someone who has even more passion for them than I!

I must also, as always, acknowledge the wonderful work from Green Ink Proofreading, which caught any number of errors and oversights in my writing and improved the initial work sufficiently to present it to you.

Finally, my eternal gratitude to Lia London, who provided critical feedback and helped me to make this a far better story than it would have been without her input. My friend Malia Laughton assisted in this regard, as well - thank you!

Errors, omissions, and oversights remain as always, my own.

Thank You

I deeply appreciate you spending the past couple of hundred pages with the characters and events of a world long past, yet hopefully relevant today.

If you enjoyed this book, I'd also be grateful for a kind review on your favorite bookseller's Web site or social media outlet. Word of mouth is the best way to make me successful, so that I can bring you even more high-quality stories of bygone times.

I'd love to hear directly from you, too—feel free to reach out to me via my Facebook page, Twitter feed, or Web site and let me know what you liked, and what you would like me to work on more.

Again, thank you for reading, for telling your friends about this book, for giving it as a gift or dropping off a copy in your favorite classroom or library. With your support and encouragement, we'll find even more times and places to explore together.

larsdhhedbor.com
Facebook: LarsDHHedbor
@LarsDHHedbor on Twitter

Enjoy a preview of the next book in the *Tales From a Revolution* series:

The Tree

The kettle was steaming and the meal had softened enough to eat before Abe's father spoke. "Working out at the edge of the big clearing today. You'd best stay clear. Plenty to do here."

"Yes, sir," Abe said, hiding his irritation. While he had no desire to work on his father's crew, he didn't like being treated as though he was his father's housewife, responsible for all of the household chores in his mother's absence.

He spooned out his serving of gruel and sat down at the heavy table to eat. The pail sat beside the hearth, leaking the last of the hard-won water out onto the floor. He'd have to clean the mess that left, in addition to the rest of the ordinary daily work.

Slurping at his gruel, he looked over at the sack that held the dried beef he'd bought a fortnight prior. While he knew that his father would scowl at the extravagance, he decided to make a stew with it for supper. There were a few onions left, and he thought he might even be able to shake a bit of flour out of the cask to thicken it. It would be nice, though, to have a few other staples.

It was too cold to bathe in the creek, and he was just as glad for that. He ran his fingers through his hair, thinking that it might be time to cut it again. Or, he thought, he could just keep his hat on his head when he was out in public, and let it go a bit longer.

"Might I have some money for eggs?" His old aunt—his

father's sister—kept an unruly flock of chickens in town, and had offered him a handsome price the last time he'd passed by. He thought he might be able to get her to go even lower, if he sweet-talked her enough. Like her brother, though, she was usually taciturn and dour, so it was hard to predict.

His father grunted, "What for?"

"Thought they'd be a nice break from the gruel. The meal's mostly gone, anyway, so I should get some more soon, and flour besides." Abe marveled at his boldness, even as he cringed inwardly in expectation of his father's inevitable explosion.

Instead, his father sighed. "I suppose. You ain't getting any smaller. Got to eat. Soon I'll start showing you the trade, need your strength for that." He passed over a handful of coins.

"Tell my sister hello for me."

Abe took the money, saying, "Yes, sir." He didn't think that the old woman would much care whether he conveyed his father's greetings or not, but he also knew that there was every chance that if he failed to do so, his father would learn of it somehow, and that would be just yet another failure for which he could be berated.

Cyrus Sawyer stood from the table, slurping down the last of his tea, and dashing the dregs into the fire, where they hissed and popped. He set the cup down on the table, swept his shaggy hair back, and slipped his work hat firmly over his head.

"Mind yourself in town, son," he said, pausing briefly at the door to look at Abe. Already taking his father's cup from the table to wash it, Abe nodded, and didn't even look up until after the door had swung closed with a bang.

He finished tidying up, deciding that the water by the hearth would dry by itself. He banked the fire and donned his hat and jacket, picking up the pail and dipper again. The air had warmed as the sun climbed the sky, and birdsong along the track toward the village made it seem almost more like springtime than the early days of autumn.

The first hint of fall's riotous colors of the hills around the house, though, revealed the season too clearly for any mere birds' singing to overcome. He returned to the stream and dipped out enough water to soak the beef in, shaking his head at the degree to which the ice had already melted away from the edges of the hole he'd made.

Pouring the water into the raised spider and setting it over the banked fire to just warm it, he pulled out the dried beef and dropped it in. Satisfied, he swung his rucksack over his shoulder and went back out into the bright sunshine and started for the village. He jingled the money in his coin purse, and wished that he could afford some squash, but that was a battle for another day. Today, he would get just the flour, meal, and eggs, and he knew that his father's flinty figuring would leave him no money for any other luxuries.

He decided to go first to the mercantile for the meal and flour. No sense in chancing the fragile eggs to more travel than was strictly necessary, and he knew, too, that there was always a chance that his aunt would be in a rare talkative mood, and he wanted to be sure that he wasn't held up so long that Mister Harper at the mercantile was already gone for the afternoon.

On the porch at Harper's, there was one of the usual pairs of bored old men, perusing the same old broadsides from down in Boston or Philadelphia, and arguing over their content. As Abe came within earshot, he could hear that the perennial topic of Governor Wentworth's unwelcome energy of late in regard to surveying and inspecting lumber. He stopped just within earshot, interested in hearing the inevitable argument.

"Those accursed surveyors little Johnny has been sending around to lay a measuring rod on every plank and log have been threatening to put the mark on any lumber they like," one old man said, spitting onto the street for emphasis.

"Nay, not just any," said another, holding his hands up in a placating gesture. "The timber or boards must be plainly in violation of the King's Mark."

His interlocutor spat again. "And once the mark is set upon the lumber, the sheriff seizes it up, and the owner of the sawmill must pay whatever fine he cares to assess, else say farewell to their lumber and their profits, easy as kiss your hand." He lifted the back of his hand to his lips and tossed it by way of demonstration.

Again the other man shook his head. "Now, Ephram, you know that ain't true. The fines are assessed according to the law, which states what fine should be laid on what size timber, all orderly and reasonable-like."

Ephram grumbled, "All I can say is that I liked Governor Wentworth's uncle better, when he were Governor over this colony. He was a right reasonable fellow, and tended to his own affairs. Up here in the woods, I like swamp law better'n any mast law, and it troubles me to hear you argue against that, Amos."

"Have a care, Ephram. If we push the Governor too far, it will give the Parliament cause to tighten the screws even further."

"Let them try," Ephram exploded. "What good is it to grant a man a parcel of land, and then deny him the blessings of that soil?"

"'Tis but a condition of that grant," Amos said calmly.

"That condition should be set upon the grant, not changed at a whim later. And when we must beg for the surveyor's deputy to find the time to come and tell us what we may and may not use from our own land, while fallen timber rots and is wasted, I suppose that you call that but a condition, as well?"

Ephram scowled at the other man, glaring at him until Amos finally shook his head and said, "We are here at the sufferance of the King and Parliament. If you like a grant that you may do with as you please, why not prove out a nice farm instead? I'm sure that you could get Governor Wentworth to make you a nice offer, given enough of an inducement."

Ephram said nothing in reply, but only spat a third time, rounding on Abe. "You, there. Your Pap, he works that grant of his and has to leave whole stands of trees be, even when experience shows that no more that one out of every twenty will ever be fit for the King's purposes. How does he like that?"

Abe was startled and alarmed to be drawn into the argument. "Well, uh, to be honest, he hasn't said, at least not anywhere that I could hear him."

"Aye, well that one don't say much where anyone can hear him. You got business with Harper, then?"

"Yes, sir," Abe said, walking around the two men. He thought he saw Amos giving him a sympathetic look as he passed.

The merchant was glad enough to see him, though he didn't seem in much of a mood to dicker over prices. In the end, though, Abe was able to purchase the flour he wanted, and even a little more meal than he had anticipated. Perhaps he could make somewhat bigger servings of gruel than usual, and his father would be well enough satisfied that Abe had made a good bargain.

By the time he came out, his rucksack bulging with the supplies he'd purchased, the old men were much more amicably discussing the shortcomings of Governor Clinton over in New-York. On that question they apparently had no significant disagreement.

The sun had risen high into the sky, and he was feeling warmed through for the first time since he'd left the kitchen that morning. The songbirds were still out in force, calling back and forth to one another, telling stories of love and desire, possession and warning.

One tree in particular seemed laden down with their tiny bodies, the noise almost deafening as Abe passed underneath. He skirted around the outer boundary of the canopy, not wishing to become as decorated as the ground under it was.

From the other side of the road, he felt a chill come over him as he heard the deep croaking call of the raven, and as he spotted the fell bird sitting on the branch of a tree there, he almost wished that he had chanced the songbirds instead. The black-feathered creature regarded him as he passed, its head cocking from side to side.

When Abe had passed by without acknowledging the raven, it hopped into the air and perched on the next tree along his route, again uttering a hoarse croak at him. Abe glared at it now and while he couldn't be sure that it was the same animal that had been present in the graveyard when his mother had been laid to rest, something made him feel certain that it was.

The creature's repeated calls and bobbing head seemed almost provocative to him, daring him to respond. He stooped and picked up a pebble to toss at the unwelcome creature. The bird clearly understood what his intention was, and flapped away, calling out disapprovingly as it went. Abe let the pebble drop back to the road and continued, shaking his head at the creature's antics.

The rest of the walk to his aunt's house was without incident, at least, and he was soon walking through the crowd of chickens that stood like guards before the gate to his aunt's house. He knew from experience that there was no point in trying to avoid the birds—they would get out of his way on their own as he walked through the flock.

These birds, at least threatened neither his hat nor his calm, and he was at his aunt's door without delay. As he raised his hand to rap at the door, it flew open, and his aunt stood there, weeping openly, and Abe just stood there dumbfounded at the sight.

She gathered him into her arms, sobbing so hard that he could scarcely understand her. "Oh, you poor boy. You poor, poor lad. I don't know how we're going to make it all work, but I will do what I can for you."

Abe pulled away, bewildered. "Aunt Rosanna, what are you talking about? All I need is some eggs for my father's breakfast tomorrow."

She wailed aloud and dragged him back into a damp embrace. When she could speak somewhat coherently again, she said, "Oh, my poor Abimael, you don't know yet, do you? Your father was struck down by a falling tree, and died instantly. You are an orphan, and will be in my care from this day forward."

Look for* The Tree: Tales From a Revolution - New-Hampshire *at your favorite booksellers.

Made in the USA
Middletown, DE
21 May 2023

31114440R00130